TWISTED

TWISTED

A Novel by
David Robbins

Based on the Motion Picture Screenplay by
Sarah Thorp

AN ONYX BOOK

ONYX
Published by New American Library, a division of
Penguin Group (USA) Inc., 375 Hudson Street,
New York, New York 10014, U.S.A.
Penguin Books Ltd, 80 Strand,
London WC2R 0RL, England
Penguin Books Australia Ltd, 250 Camberwell Road,
Camberwell, Victoria 3124, Australia
Penguin Books Canada Ltd, 10 Alcorn Avenue,
Toronto, Ontario, Canada M4V 3B2
Penguin Books (N.Z.) Ltd, Cnr Rosedale and Airborne Roads,
Albany, Auckland 1310, New Zealand

Penguin Books Ltd, Registered Offices:
80 Strand, London WC2R 0RL, England

Published by Onyx, an imprint of New American Library,
a division of Penguin Group (USA) Inc.

First Printing, February 2004
10   9   8   7   6   5   4   3   2   1

CHAPTER 1

The morning sun blazed bright over the Golden Gate Bridge and the traffic streaming across it. Seagulls glided on outstretched wings over the bay. Closer to shore, near San Francisco's waterfront, sea lions plied the water with graceful ease.

Beyond the waterfront was an abandoned industrial area, its squat buildings dark and grim, its shadowed alleys mired in gloom. A stiff breeze off the bay stirred the trash that littered the ground: candy wrappers, fast food containers, all the usual residue of human sloth.

Inside a grimy building at the north end of the industrial park, it was darker than in the alleys. Dark and still . . . so still that Jessica Shepard heard the quick breaths she was taking. Fear was the catalyst— fear she was struggling to control. She felt a bead of sweat trickle down her cheek. The next instant she felt something else—the razor-sharp tip of a knife breaking the skin at the base of her throat.

"I can hear your heart beating," Eddy Culter taunted. He was behind her, his body pressed tight against hers. "Can you?"

Yes, Jess could, but she refused to answer.

"It sounds like a little animal in your chest trying to get out," Eddy said.

Jess involuntarily tensed when his free hand roved under her black leather jacket and pried at her white tank top.

"It sounds like flesh."

Rough fingers cupped a breast, and Jessica's breath caught in her throat.

"But most of all," Eddy said, "it sounds like love."

Eddy's rough hand strayed lower. Jess readied herself. Suddenly, he was the one who tensed. "Hey. What in the hell is this?"

"Why, that's my gun," Jess said. Her training kicked in. She elbowed him in the gut to buy herself room even as she grabbed the wrist of his knife hand and twisted it hard enough to elicit a yelp of pain. She continued twisting, set her shoulder into his armpit, and executed a flawless flip.

Culter sailed up and over and hit the cement with a thud. The knife went skidding into the shadows.

In a blur, Jess drew her Beretta and gouged it

against his cheek. "On your knees!" she ordered. "Now! Do it, damn you!"

"Okay! Okay!" Eddy whined. "Please don't hurt me." He knelt, quaking with fright, his head bowed low.

Continuing to press her pistol against him, Jess whipped her cellular phone from a jacket pocket and used the speed dial. When a voice answered, she said crisply, "Wilson, I need backup. Twenty-three Rolfton Street. The old Battery."

Eddy twisted his head, mewing, "Can't you take this thing out of my face? You're hurting me."

"Shut up!" Jess barked. "Hands behind your head!"

He hesitated.

"Do it, damn you! Or so help me—"

"All right." Eddy slowly raised his hands.

"Do it faster!" Jess half expected him to try something. Most of them did once they were caught. The rabbit syndrome, it was called, a common trait among perps of all kinds. She jammed the pistol harder.

"I am! I am!"

Jess warily slipped behind him and expertly cuffed him. Only when the handcuffs were secure did she step back away and allow herself to relax. From the speaker on her cell phone blared the voice of her partner.

"Ten-Four. Backup units rolling. Code Three. Hold him there, Jessica."

Eddy Culter was pouting. "You're a cop?"

"Just your luck, huh?" Jess moved back around in front of him.

Eddy looked her up and down, and leered. His laugh was cold and brittle.

"Oh, yeah. One more thing," Jess said, and kicked him in the face.

Dr. Melvin Frank, the police psychiatrist, was known for his results, but not necessarily his attention to ancillary things that got results. Degrees and commendations lined his walls, but his desk was drowning in paperwork. The same fate that must have met the dead fish in his tank, although technically, Jess thought, fish probably didn't drown. Whatever. She shifted to make herself more comfortable on his couch.

"Nerves bothering you?" Dr. Frank asked.

"Never better," Jess replied.

"Any nightmares?"

Jessica kept her voice level and replied simply, "Nope."

"Or insomnia? Anxiety? Panic attacks?" Dr. Frank smiled.

"Nope. Nada." Jess didn't look at him when she said it. He could be annoyingly perceptive.

"It must have been scary," Frank commented.

"Not really," Jess searched for the right word. "It was exhilarating."

"Exhilarating? To kick him?"

"No, it was exhilarating to catch him," Jess clarified. She had an unlit cigarette in her hand and rolled it from finger to finger, a habit she couldn't break.

Dr. Frank sighed. "Okay, here's the deal. This session is mandated. It's standard procedure for any cop who's been through a traumatic experience. Plus, in this instance, the suspect got a little roughed up."

"No. Really?" Jess said with more than a touch of sarcasm.

"A tiny voice inside of me tells me that you're not cooperating as fully as you should."

Jessica grinned. "Hear voices a lot, do you?"

"Jess, you need to take this seriously." Dr. Frank tapped his temple. "Anything you tell me goes into the vault. Unless I'm convinced a crime is about to be committed. In which case, I'm legally obligated to inform the department." When she didn't say anything, he went on. "Let's get something straight. I'm not the enemy. I don't have a dog in this fight. A cop gets in harm's way, he can get a little chewed up."

"Or *she*," Jess stressed.

"Right. Or *she* can get chewed up. Your promotion is not in jeopardy."

"Good to know," Jess said coldly. "Anything else?"

"Anything you need to get off your chest?"

"You're really hoping I've got some big problems. You work on commission?"

"Believe me or not, I care about the welfare of my patients. And to answer your question, I prefer to find people in perfect mental health."

"Well, then, Doc, say hello to Perfect Mental Health."

"Really? And how do you rationalize kicking the suspect when he was helpless?"

Jessica rolled the cigarette faster. "You gotta get physical every once in a while."

"What's 'once in a while'?"

Jess sat up. "Look. You've been on the street. You know what it's like, all the hell we go through. John Q. Public thinks we're robots. Thinks we can wallow in violence and not let it get to us. But that's not how it works. We're human. We have feelings."

Dr. Frank grinned. "Thank you."

"For what?"

"For finally opening up to me."

"Then I can go?" Jess shot to her feet.

The psychiatrist's grin widened. "Not hardly. We're just getting started."

A cop by the name of Quinlan had built the bar a decade before Jessica was born, but he was still there, still serving drinks and rubbing elbows with the people he loved most in the world: other cops.

On this particular night the music was blaring as

loud as ever, and the place was crowded from wall to wall. There were cops at the bar, cops in the booths. There were cops playing pool, cops throwing darts. Some in uniform, some in street clothes. A boisterous babble fell on Jess's ears as she opened the door and strolled in.

"Well, look who it is!"

Jess had hardly taken two steps when she was seized in powerful arms and whisked in a dance in rhythm to a song blaring on the jukebox. The arms were steady, but the feet were a little wobbly. She smiled and flowed with the music, and tried to steady the big man who had commanded her attention. "Hey, partner. Or should I say *ex*-partner?"

"Hey, yourself." Wilson Jefferson's teeth were white against his black skin. "That was some bust."

"It was dumb luck," Jess said.

"Never sell yourself short, babe," Wilson advised. "There are too many others always willing to do that for us."

A voice boomed from a stool at the bar. "Hey! Shepard! Do that thing again!"

Jess half turned. "Aw, come on," she protested. They had been having her do it every night for a week. But that was a dress rehearsal. Tonight she had the goods and she could show them.

"Do it! Do it!" the instigator chanted, and the refrain was taken up by a dozen others.

She was outnumbered by big, burly cops. She sighed. She'd have to give in. Truth was, she couldn't wait. Pulling out her new badge, Jess spun around and struck a pose. In an overly dramatic voice, she announced, "Inspector Shepard, Homicide!"

There was good-natured laughter and someone called out, "Do it again! This time show some boob!"

"Like hell." Jess replaced her badge. "Beers?"

A few heads bobbed.

"They're on me," Jess offered, and couldn't help laughing at the stampede it caused. "Yeah, that's what I thought, you cheap bastards!"

"Three cheers for Jess!" someone whooped.

Shouldering her way to the bar, Jessica motioned for Quinlan, who indicated he would be with her in a minute. She placed her elbows on the bar and was bobbing her head to the music when an arm slipped around her shoulders.

"You see? You and me"—Wilson crossed his fingers and held them in front of her eyes—"we're like this. You know what?"

Jess pretended to think really hard, then snapped her fingers. "Umm . . . you're drunk."

Wilson sniffed in mock indignation. "Just because you're moving up to Homicide, don't take me off your speed dial. Anytime you press that button, I'll be waiting at the other end." He downed some of his drink and sadly regarded her. "I'm going to miss you."

"I'm gonna miss you, too, Wilson," Jess said, and meant it. They had worked well together.

"Fuck that sentimental shit." Wilson straightened. "I'm trying to tell you these Homicide guys are mental. They're turned on by fucking corpses."

A handsome Puerto Rican guy Jess had never seen before was walking past and overheard the remark. "Really?"

Wilson had to squint to see him, he was so plastered. "What the fuck's that? The peanut gallery?"

"I was just wondering. Do you mean they're turned on by fucking *corpses* or by *fucking* corpses?"

"What we've got here is a smart-ass," Wilson said.

"Hey, you don't want people to hear you, you shouldn't talk so loud" was the guy's retort.

Jess sensed a potential brawl. She grabbed several bottles of beer. "Hey, Wilson. Let's pass beers out."

"Sure," Wilson said, and turned away.

After a few moments of confusion, with everyone grabbing for a bottle at once, Jess faced the new guy, who was leaning on the bar and smirking at her.

"What?" he asked.

"Nothing. I'm just thinking about how you must have a death wish."

"Why? Because I razzed your friend? He's a big boy. He can take it." The guy paused and sized up his adversary. "You think this isn't my kind of place?"

"I know it isn't," Jess flatly stated. She was casing him right back. "Even though you are a cop."

"Is it that obvious?"

"No. I'm just that good," Jessica said matter-of-factly. "What precinct are you in?"

The guy didn't say anything.

"What? It's top secret?" Jess baited him, miffed by the cold shoulder. "Whatever floats your boat." She made for the jukebox and fished in her pocket for change.

"Hey, sexy," someone said almost in her ear.

"Hey, Jimmy," Jess said, wishing it were anyone but him. She had been doing her best to avoid him for more than two weeks.

Despite a nose that had been broken twice in fights, Jimmy Schmidt was still undeniably good-looking. He was still in his patrol uniform, his badge glinting on his broad chest. "I've missed you," he said, and reached for her. "How about a dance?"

Jess dodged his hand. "No, thanks."

"Oooh. Chilly," Jimmy carped.

"Jimmy, please. I just want to enjoy myself tonight, okay?" Jess said.

"Me, too." Jimmy said. "I even have something for you."

"Really? What?" Jess's surprise was no sham. He had never been the considerate type.

"This." Jimmy flipped her the finger, then laughed and lowered it. "I'm sorry. Seriously, I'm happy for you."

"Sure you are," Jess said, looking past Jimmy, where she saw a well-dressed middle-aged man saunter into the bar as if he, and not Fred Quinlan, were the owner. A path automatically opened for him as he came straight toward her and Schmidt.

Jimmy had his back to the newcomer and was saying, "I just wish *my* mentor was a police commissioner. Maybe then I'd be getting a promotion, too."

"Is that so?" the man asked. He had a booming bass voice that instantly commanded attention.

Whirling, Jimmy took a step back. "Commissioner Mills, sir!"

"I've got ears like a cat, son," John Mills said. He was smiling, but the smile didn't reach his eyes. "Let's see what we can do about getting you that promotion. Test." He folded his arms across his chest. "There's a man sitting at the end of the bar behind you. Looks like he's been there all night. Describe him. I want detail."

Jimmy nervously shifted his weight from one foot to the other. "Naw. Forget it. I'm just here to have a good time."

"Talking to me isn't your idea of a good time? I'm hurt," Mills said. "Or maybe you just can't do it?"

The room had gone quiet and all eyes were on the commissioner and the patrolman.

A red tinge bloomed on Jimmy's cheeks. "Of course I can do it." He started to turn toward the man at the bar, but Mills stepped between them, blocking his view.

"Uh-uh. Look at me."

"Sure, whatever you say." Beads of sweat had broken out on Jimmy's brow. "Uhhh, let's see. He's a white guy. Dark hair. Dark jacket." He knew he was beat. Jimmy wasn't playing anymore. "Whatever, man. I'm off duty."

Mills's assessment of Jimmy was verified. "Right. Shepard?" Jess hesitated. The crowd sat in rapt silence. "You don't know?" Mills taunted.

Then Jess rattled it off with machine gun cadence. "White male, late forties, brown hair, blue eyes, one hundred and sixty pounds, brown sports jacket, wedding ring, gold chain with some sort of medallion around his neck. He's been paying cash and he's on his fifth shot."

Jimmy blushed deeper.

Commissioner Mills poked him in the chest. "That's why she got the promotion and not you. A real inspector is never off duty." He winked at Jess. "My office."

Although it pleased Jessica no end to see Jimmy put in his place, she felt uncomfortable about being the vehicle of his embarrassment and looked back to say she hoped there were no hard feelings.

Jimmy Schmidt was glaring at her and clenching and unclenching his big fists, almost as if he yearned to wrap his hands around her neck and strangle her until she was dead, dead, dead.

CHAPTER 2

The back room of the bar was reserved for billiards. Four tables were lined up two by two, their felt maintained in top condition, new chalk set out every day. A lot of officers took their pool playing seriously and had customized sticks in racks on the wall.

Commissioner Mills hung his coat on a peg and claimed the chair always reserved for him in a far corner, where he could watch the matches. He opened a humidor on a stand beside the chair and helped himself to an expensive cigar. Taking out a folding knife, he clipped the cigar, palmed a lighter, and went through the ritual of lighting the cigar, puffing until it caught.

Smiling happily, Jess patiently waited. For the first time in more days than she could remember, she was genuinely happy. But it wouldn't last. It never did.

"Well," Mills said, puffing a cloud large enough to engulf the city, "how about that? Inspector Shepard. Making an old man proud." He examined the glowing end of his cigar. "You passed the written?"

"I aced it," Jess bragged. "How could I not? I've learned from the master."

"Really? I can hardly believe how badly you almost fucked it up."

The abrupt change in his tone startled her. Jess could only blurt, "What?"

"A moment ago you demonstrated that you still know how to process a room," Mills observed. It was a compliment, but he scowled when he said it, turning it into an admonition. Mills jabbed his cigar at her. "So let me ask you this: how did this psychopath get a knife to your throat?"

Her knees went weak and Jess leaned on the pool table, fighting down a rising tide of terror. She didn't dare tell him. He would never understand her secret. Not in a million years.

"Let me tell you. You went there alone. Without backup. Without telling anybody. You didn't follow procedure and you almost got yourself killed."

"I'd say you're as good as ever," Jess said, although it couldn't be further from the truth.

"Stupid, stupid, stupid," Mills said in disgust. "I thought I taught you better. You're lucky you're not being pulled in for disciplinary review instead of being promoted."

"You're absolutely right."

"Lesson learned," Mills said, and visibly soft-ened. "You made it through okay. You were lucky. But you're Homicide now. No more room for mis-takes. Okay?"

"Okay," she assured him.

Rising, Mills affectionately chucked her on the chin with his fist, doing it so gently he barely touched her. "Good." He winked. "Nice kick, by the way."

Jess laughed, as much from relief as from his quip.

"Now quit wasting your time with an old fart like me and go party hearty." Mills gave her a light push.

The rest of the evening was vastly more pleas-ant. Jessica had two drinks, enough to give her a nice buzz, but not enough to muddy her thinking. She talked with friends, played a game of darts. But the whole time an unwanted familiar feeling grew deep inside her—a feeling she dreaded, but could no more deny than she could the impulse to breathe. It got so bad by nine, she went into the ladies' room to splash water on her face and get her act together, even though it was a lost cause.

Mills was by the bar holding court when she came out. "I mean," he said to his audience, "what kind of moron tries to flush body parts down the toilet? There was a furnace right out back."

At the howls of mirth, Jess tapped him on the shoulder. "I'm gonna go."

"Hey, get over here. What are you doing hiding? This is your night." Mills grabbed her hand and turned her to the crowd. "The department's first female police chief, right here! You just watch."

Three men around Mills toasted Jess. A female officer did a deep curtsy, and howls rose to the ceiling.

"God, you remind me of your father," Mills said. "He would have been so proud of you. Now go straight home and get some sleep. You have a big day tomorrow."

"I will," Jessica lied. She was halfway to the door when she saw the new guy at the piano. He wasn't half bad. He nodded at her, but after how rudely he'd treated her, she didn't return the courtesy. Instead, she marched out into the cool of the night and stood for a minute breathing deep and trying, yet again, to smother the need that had taken control of her.

She glanced back as she went up the street and saw the new guy in front of the bar, staring. If he followed her she'd have to do something about it, but he seemed stuck to that spot. Good. She hurried to her next destination.

Twice Jessica felt she was being followed. The first time she shrugged it off as jitters. The second time she ducked into a recessed doorway and stayed there for more than two minutes, but no one came along she would peg as suspicious.

*   *   *

The Saloon on Northbeach was the haunt of the mostly young and the mostly restless. They came there for only one reason. Shadowy nooks hid hunched figures. Conversations were conducted in whispers. On the dance floor, couples were entwined like vines.

Jess found her usual seat empty. The bartender brought her usual drink and placed a napkin under it. "Thanks."

"Bottoms up."

Taking a sip, Jess surveyed her prospects. A yuppie at the other end smiled at her, but yuppies had a tendency to be interested only in getting their own jollies. A kid who looked barely old enough to shave eyed her from across the room, but she wasn't into charity cases.

Then a rock-and-roll type in a leather jacket a lot like hers strutted toward her. He had an air of recklessness about him. When he leaned down she saw a large tattoo of a musical note on his hand. They locked eyes and she sensed he was trying to come up with something clever to introduce himself. She made it easy. "You live around here?"

Jess didn't introduce herself. She never did anymore. It was only four blocks to his apartment, which was just as well because the two of them were smoldering volcanoes by then and couldn't keep their hands off each other.

Once they were inside, it was a blur of lips and hands and clothes flying. Jess let herself go. She needed the release as much if not more than he did, and she savored every second of the long carnal climb to the summit.

Then came the descent to earth. Jess started to dress and moved to the window to scan the street. It was well past midnight and the neighborhood was in for the night. She heard him in the bathroom, heard water run. The door opened and he came up behind her.

For a shockingly clear instant, Jess could see his reflection in the window. It wasn't the rock and roller—it was Edmund Culter, and he was leering suggestively. His hand reached for her. At the contact, she jumped and came close to drawing her gun.

"What's wrong?"

"Nothing," Jessica lied for the second time in as many hours.

"So my name's Larry. What's yours?"

"I have to go." Jess deflated his bubble. She avoided looking at him as she finished dressing.

"I hope we can do this again sometime."

"We won't." Jess left and, once she reached the sidewalk, broke into a jog. She couldn't wait to get to her own apartment. At the corner, she hesitated. Again her intuition was blaring. She swore unseen eyes were upon her. Although she had scoured every dark nook and sheltered cranny, she saw no one.

"I'm getting worse all the time," Jess said. Her

nerves continued to jangle until she was safe behind her own door, which she locked and bolted. She slid several CDs into the CD player, then walked to the kitchen, passing a large photo of herself and Commissioner Mills—Mills with his arm on her shoulder, both of them smiling.

From a cupboard above the stove, Jess took a pack of herbal tea and made herself a steaming hot cup. She could use something to relax her so she could sleep. Once, the sex had been enough. But of late, the bliss lasted for shorter and shorter spans.

A rectangle of light flared in the building across from hers. Like clockwork, the old Chinese woman appeared in the window, only to quickly retreat when she saw Jess spot her.

Jess never could understand what that was all about. She had toyed with the notion the woman was spying on her, but that was absurd.

It was past two. By rights Jess should get to bed but she didn't feel tired. She went to her closet. Her uniform hung inside; above it was a stack of boxes. She had to rise onto the tips of her toes to reach the one she wanted.

Gingerly, reverently, Jess set it on the floor and curled her legs under her. "Been a while," she said softly.

Inside were some of her most prized possessions. On top was the Raggedy Ann doll she'd had as a girl. Taking it out, she cradled it, then smiled, awash in happy memories. "Too bad we can't stay young forever," she wistfully remarked.

Underneath was a pink ribbon. Jess fondled it, recalling when her mother had given it to her. "Oh, Mom," she said, and kissed the ribbon as lovingly as she would have kissed her mother were her mother alive.

Her high school class ring, her yearbook, and a plastic cup and saucer from the Playtime Tea Set were next. She fondly caressed a crushed rose a boy had given her at her first dance. It had been preserved in a plastic bag.

"Yesterday," Jess said, then shuddered. She had glimpsed the contents at the bottom: old newspaper clippings and photographs of bloody bodies.

Quickly, Jess replaced everything and put the box up on the shelf. Shuffling to the bed, she stripped and flopped down, relishing the softness of the quilt and the pillow. She thought of Larry and wondered what he would tell his friends. Then she thought of Mills, and his pride in her promotion. She smiled, then scowled as the image of the guy at the bar filled her mind. Why did he follow her outside? What was his game?

That was the last thought she had until the break of day and the jangle of her alarm.

Her weekday morning ritual began with a visit to the Palace of Fine Arts. Tai chi practitioners were going through various movements. Another group practiced with Asian swords.

Jess donned her sweatsuit and did her warm-up exercises, then joined some of her fellow officers for a training session with their *yawara* instructor. She never ceased to be amazed at how effective the batonlike weapon was; in skilled hands, it could take down opponents in any number of ways. Nerve center strikes were the focus for today, and for an hour she practiced the routines under the instructor's watchful eye.

Next came yoga class. Jess liked yoga because it loosened her joints and made her arms and legs more flexible. She also liked to read as she stretched. Today, it was the *SFPD Training Manual*, Yawara, *Nonlethal Offensive Weapon*.

Afterward, Jess was more than ready to hit the showers. A quick rush home to dress for work, and she would be on her way. She didn't want to be late on her first day at her new job. Double-checking herself in the full-length mirror in the bathroom, she nodded. "You go, girl," she said with as much confidence as she could muster.

The Homicide Division was on the second floor. Jess climbed the stairs slowly, a swarm of butterflies loose in her stomach. She came to the door, took a deep breath, and plunged on in.

Bedlam ran rampant. Detectives were everywhere. On the phone, taking reports, typing at their computers, laughing, shouting, eating. Crime scene photos, some depicting the most gruesome scenes imaginable, covered the walls.

Jess let the chaos wash over her and stepped to a nearby desk. A secretary in her late forties was trying to talk on the phone, type, and file her nails, all at the same time.

"Hi. I'm looking for Inspector Delmarco."

"About?"

"I'm his new partner."

For some reason the secretary snickered, then threw back her head and bellowed like a drill sergeant, "Delmarco? Where the hell is Delmarco?" To Jess she said, "He hasn't checked out, so he should be floating around here somewhere. It shouldn't be long."

"Thanks."

The secretary swiveled her chair toward her computer. "I was right. There he is now."

To say Jess was surprised was an understatement. The guy crossing the room was her mystery man from the previous night. "You've got to be kidding me."

"Do I look like the kidding type?" the secretary asked.

Mike Delmarco was moving toward a bulletin board. One of the other detectives spotted him and called out, "Thumb tacks!"

"He needs thumb tacks?" Jess asked.

"No, hon, it's a game they play. Give a listen."

Delmarco broke stride, thoughtfully tapped his

chin, and smiled. "Lancaster, Pennsylvania. A seventy-year-old man was convicted of murdering his wife of fifty years by putting thumb tacks in her breakfast cereal. Said he couldn't stand the noises she made while she ate." He pinned a photo to the bulletin board, then came toward the front desk.

"Try me. Pick an object. Any object. If I can't come up with a murder case in which the object was used, you win."

"Thanks. I'll pass."

He made an attempt at an introduction. Not much of an attempt, but that was his style.

"Delmarco. Follow me." But he took only a few steps before stopping and raising his voice. "Boys, say hello to Inspector Shepard."

Every detective looked. Jess tried not to be embarrassed, but she felt like a microbe under a microscope.

They continued on. Mike halted between two desks and patted the one on the right. Behind it sat a bull of a man with a thick neck and a perpetual frown. "Meet Dale Becker." He patted the empty desk on the left. "This one is yours."

"Well, well, what have we here?" Dale said.

"Inspector Shepard. I'm partnering up with Inspector Delmarco." Jess set him straight, and couldn't understand why Becker gave her a look of sheer disgust. She'd barely known him five seconds.

"Well, Shepard, here's a tip for you," Dale said,

speaking loudly so everyone could hear. "Stumbling on a suspect does not an inspector make. Good luck, honey."

"I never claimed it did," Jess said, defending herself, and regretting it when his mouth curled in a sneer.

"Someone must think so." Becker's grin was sarcasm personified. "I wonder who that could be."

Jess looked to Mike for a little help.

"Dale was primary on the Culter thing," he whispered. "Then you waltz in with the suspect. You've got enemies already. So you ready to work?"

"Yep."

Mike chortled, then snagged some files from another desk, apparently his own. "Congratulations! Welcome to Homicide."

Mike led her to the lieutenant's office and entered without knocking. Hunched over his desk with a phone to his ear was a man who looked as if his day had started off bad and gotten progressively worse. He was angry, and he gestured at them to wait.

"Okay. Okay. I'm hanging up now," the lieutenant rasped into the phone. "No, listen . . ."

Jess leaned toward Mike. "Maybe we should come back."

"Why? This is one of his good moods."

The lieutenant kept on arguing with whoever was on the other end. Jess gave the office a once-over, but in reality she was studying her new partner. He was undeniably handsome, in a rugged way. Abruptly, she realized he had caught her scoping him out and he was grinning at her expense. To cover herself she whispered, "Grapefruits."

"What?"

"Murder weapon."

Mike pursed his lips. "Ummm, let me see. New York City. August, nineteen seventy-eight. A man drops a grapefruit off an eight-story building. It hits his boss on the head. His boss falls and cracks his head open on the sidewalk."

He grinned and she grinned and then someone coughed.

"How nice," the lieutenant said. "Well, I see you two have already developed a rapport. Wonderful." He thrust a hand toward Jessica. "Lieutenant Tabor, in case our walking encyclopedia failed to mention it."

"Sir," Jess said, shaking his hand.

"Just do us all a favor," the lieutenant said, eyeing the new partners.

"Yes, sir." Jess was eager to please.

"Please don't sleep together. It'll save everyone a lot of headaches."

CHAPTER 3

Jessica Shepard was no different from any other woman. She had been dealing with the "gender thing," as she'd dubbed it, since she was old enough to remember. Dealing with the stares. The innuendos. The crude comments. With being treated as a sex object instead of a person. She resented it, as any thinking woman did, but the only solution was to wipe the opposite gender off the face of the planet, which was a tad extreme, in her estimation.

Men couldn't help being "male." Most simply didn't know any better. They didn't realize they were doing anything wrong. Not all men were that way, thank God, but enough to make life a constant trial.

One aspect of police work Jess liked was that the sexism was held to a minimum. It wasn't that cops were inherently more sensitive than the male population at large. It was the job. Men and women putting their lives on the line each and every day. As partners. As comrades in arms. As equals. In an environment like that, the usual distinctions no longer existed. Women were accepted for *who* they were rather than *what* they were.

So Lieutenant Tabor's comment came as even more of a shock to Jess. All she could do was stare, unsure whether he was crude or insensitive or both.

Mike said out of the corner of his mouth, "Don't mind him. Messy divorce."

To Jess, that hardly excused it. "My personal life is my own, sir. I don't see where who I sleep with is of any importance."

Tabor leaned on his desk and wearily regarded her. "That's where you're wrong, Inspector. Because nine times out of ten when two detectives sleep together, it spills over into their work and causes no end of headaches for me. Do I look like I need more headaches in my life?"

"No," Jess admitted. He looked like he carried the weight of the world on his shoulders.

"All I'm saying is that I expect a certain degree of professionalism from my people. I'm sorry if it came out wrong." Tabor glanced at her new partner. "Mike. Get outta here."

"Yes, sir." Mike ducked out the door.

"Close it!" Tabor commanded.

Jess heard the door shut and waited in uncomfortable silence for whatever the lieutenant had to say. She had hoped they would start off on a better footing than this.

"So. Here she is. The commissioner's pride and joy."

"I know. Listen, Lieutenant, for the record, I do not expect any special treatment."

"That's good 'cause you sure as shit aren't gonna get it. Have a seat." Lieutenant Tabor sank into his chair. He pulled a lighter from his pocket, and lit a stick of incense in an ashtray. "Ever use this stuff?"

"Sometimes," Jess said. "I like some of the scents." She never would have taken him for the kind to use it, though.

"It makes me want to puke. The lady at the corner store made me buy it, said it would calm my nerves. I'm pretty sure that the only thing that's gonna calm my nerves right now is a full frontal lobotomy."

Jess didn't know the man well enough to comment, but she was pretty sure he really didn't want her to say anything. So she just sat quietly while he continued.

Tabor had been inhaling the fumes, but now he glanced up. "My marriage is in ruins. I hardly ever get to see my kids. I'm in hock up to my armpits and I'm twenty pounds overweight from sitting on my ass all damn day and I've been skipped over for promotion twice now and I have to ride herd

over a bunch of misfits who can never seem to follow rules and regulations. But enough about me."

And he meant it. Tabor gave Jessica a long, hard
once-over look.

"From what I understand about the way you
handled that Culter thing, I don't think you're
gonna need special treatment. Am I right about
this?"

"Absolutely."

"Good. I like being right. It happens so rarely."
Tabor grinned, and Jess did, too. "Just be on time,
do your job, and try not to make my life worse than
it already is." He cocked his head and said out of
the blue, "You know, your old man was some cop
back in his day."

Caught off guard, Jess swallowed and said,
"Thank you, sir."

Tabor extended his hand. "That will be all, Inspector. Allow me to officially welcome you to
Homicide."

Mike was waiting just outside. Jess looked a little shell-shocked, but she'd obviously made it
through okay.

"You get used to him." Mike moved toward
their desks. "Well, how about I introduce you to
some of the others and walk you through the basics? Like where the coffeepot is. If you take the last
cup, make a new pot. We're detectives. We dust for
prints when we find an empty pot."

Jess smiled.

"Marge, our secretary," Mike continued the orientation, "doesn't do coffee. In fact, she doesn't do too much of anything except answer the phone and yell loud enough to be heard in New Jersey."

This time Jess actually laughed. She worried it might be the last time she'd do so in this office.

"If there's anything you want to know, all you need do is ask—okay?"

"Okay." Jess thought of something. "There is one thing."

"Shoot."

"Why didn't you say anything last night at the bar? Why didn't you tell me who you were?"

Mike stopped cold. "I couldn't. I was working a mark."

"Who?"

"You."

Jess tried to read his expression. "Why on earth would you do something like that, Inspector?"

"Self-preservation," Mike said.

"I don't follow. How could I be a danger to you?" Jess remembered her feeling of being followed, and raw fear spiked through her.

"I knew we were to be partnered up and I wanted to see you in your natural habitat. Get a handle on what kind of person you are. On how reliable you are. I'll be counting on you to cover my back and I need to be sure you'll be there for me when I need you to be."

"And you could learn all that by spying on me?"

Jess angrily asked. Her stomach balled into a knot as her suspicion grew.

"No. Of course not. But you can tell a lot about a person just by observing them. So I wanted to observe you a while before we became joined at the hip." Mike smiled. "It's nothing personal. I did the same with my last two partners."

"So how much observing did you do?"

"Sorry?"

"Did you tail me after I left the bar?" Jess kept her voice calm but only with an effort. Someone had been following her last night, and if it was him, then he had seen her go into the Saloon. And if he had seen her go in, he might have seen her come out with Larry.

"Why would I do that?"

"You tell me," Jess demanded.

"Sheathe your claws there, partner. All I was doing was checking you out. Honest to God."

Jess let it drop but her doubt lingered. Over the next hour she pumped hands and learned the office routine, but the whole time she was thinking about the Saloon and what would happen if her secret got out.

Eleven o'clock rolled around. Mike Delmarco shrugged into his jacket and said, "How about I treat you to an early lunch?"

"Can't. I have an appointment."

"With who?"

Jess had to remind herself that he wasn't being

nosy, that partners were always open with one another. "With my shrink." His eyebrows arched, so she elaborated. "The Culter thing. Department regulations."

"So you really did beat the crap out of him?"

"Just the snot, not the crap," she admitted. "They have to make sure I'm not suffering from any deep-seated traumas."

"Are you?" Mike asked.

"I'm as perfect as perfect can be," Jess said, and laughed, but it sounded hollow, even to her.

The time allotted for their session was almost over. Dr. Frank was scribbling notes on a clipboard, so Jess rose from the couch and strayed over to the fish tank. "I guess Culter did impact my life. He got me promoted. I should send him a card."

"Hmmph" was all Frank said.

"So do I pass?" Jess grinned at him.

"Almost." Dr. Frank stopped scribbling. "There is one more thing I'd like to talk about."

"Go for it. I'm an open book." Jess avoided looking at him for fear her eyes would give away the truth.

"I'd like to talk about your parents."

Jess froze. She could feel the blood drain from her face and she carefully composed herself before turning. "My parents are dead. They died in a car accident."

"Oh. Okay," Dr. Frank said. "So that's what you tell people?"

"What do you—" Jess began, and stopped when she saw a thick file resting on his leg under the clipboard. "I thought this was supposed to be about my job. I don't see how my parents relate."

"Well . . ." Dr. Frank placed the file on top of the clipboard and opened it. "Twenty-five years ago your father went on a killing spree that ended with your mother. You've devoted your life to tracking killers. You don't see how it relates? Umm, are you sure?"

"Damn you," Jess said.

"Well, that's a little less articulate than I'd like."

"I was raised by John Mills, my father's old partner. I barely remember my parents."

Dr. Frank considered this. "Okay. But it could be that your anger problems—"

Jess didn't let him finish. "I already told you. I don't *have* anger problems! I don't have any problems. I feel fantastic."

"Wow. You're lucky. What's your secret?"

"I avoid shrinks," Jess snapped. "Which reminds me, how many more of these sessions do we have to have?"

Dr. Frank let her have it smack between the eyes. "As many as I think you need. And I have to tell you, I think you need a lot."

"Based on what?" Jess was so upset, she was trembling.

"Based on how you are acting right this moment. Based on the anger that drove you to kick Edmund Culter in the face. Based on the repressed emotions I sense you have, and which shouldn't be bottled up for your own sake as well as for the sake of those around you. Do you need more?"

"No," Jess said. She had hoped that they were about done, that her past wouldn't enter into it. Because if he dug deeper, he might unearth the one thing she didn't want him to find.

"Then you can go. But make another appointment with my secretary on your way out." Frank paused. "Listen, my job is to help you deal with your feelings."

"I deal with my feelings plenty."

"Do you? I wonder. Just remember. I'm always available to talk to if you need an ear."

That will be the day, Jess thought.

That evening, alone in her apartment, Jess glumly sat at the kitchen table and poured herself a glass of wine. She needed it to relax, to warm her insides, and to help her forget about the rotten day she'd had. Dale Becker, Lieutenant Tabor, Dr. Frank, Mike Delmarco—all of them could go to hell as far as she was concerned.

She started to raise the glass, then stopped, puzzled. From outside there came a peculiar clicking noise she couldn't quite identify. It sounded close by. She glanced at her window and a tingle ran down her spine.

It was ajar! But Jess was sure it had been closed and locked when she left that morning. She always locked her windows and doors. It was second nature. Drawing her Beretta Model 96D Brigadier, she switched off the safety and cautiously moved toward the window.

The strange clicking became louder.

Crouching, Jess peered out. She couldn't see much more than the apartment across the way. Gripping the bottom of the window, she eased it open. She was trying not to make noise, but the sash was warped and suddenly there was a loud scraping sound, like fingernails on a blackboard.

Almost instantly, the clicking stopped. Jess levered the window the rest of the way and leaned out, returning her pistol to a two-handed grip. She looked up, she looked down. The fire escape was empty, fading into the darkness. No footsteps came from the alley below. There was nothing at all to indicate anyone had been there. But someone had.

In the distance a siren wailed: her brothers and sisters at work.

Slamming the window shut, Jessica locked it and pulled the curtains. She set her Beretta on the table and sat down to finish her wine. She sipped slowly, pondering. Maybe there hadn't been anyone out there at all. Maybe it was the wind. Maybe a piece of metal on the fire escape had come loose and made the noise.

Her gaze drifted to the closet. On an impulse Jess took down the big box. She placed it on her ottoman and sat next to it. The doll, the ribbons, the flower and rest, she put to one side. Then, her fingers shaking slightly, she removed the newspaper clippings and the photos.

It had been a while since Jess looked at them. A long while. She stared at a photo of her father slumped in a chair, blood running from his temple. "How could you?" she softly asked. "All those people? And then your own life?"

Jess bent over another photo. It was a close-up of an ear, and a bloody X behind it. She straightened and reached into the box and brought out several small carved wooden toys. On the bottom of each an X had been carved. "You made these with your own hands, I was told."

Another photograph caught her eye. This time it was of her mother as her mother had been twenty-five years ago: young, vibrant, smiling. The resemblance between them was striking. They looked enough alike to be twins. "Genetics will out, huh, Mom?" Jess said.

Sitting back, Jess stared longingly at the photo. Tears trickled from her eyes. "I miss you, Mom. God, how I miss the both of you."

The corners of the photo blurred and Jess uttered a soft sob and then ran her sleeve across her eyes. She stopped crying, but the blurriness was worse. She looked up and the entire room was going dark, not abruptly as it would if the lights were switched off, but slowly, gradually, like a movie fading to black.

And then she passed out.

An insistent beeping intruded on the darkness. Jess became vaguely aware of it and tried to shut it out, but it wouldn't stop, wouldn't grant her the peace she craved. With a start she realized it was her phone. Jolted awake, she glanced about in confusion. She was still fully dressed, in the exact same position she had been when she blacked out. "What in the—"

Another beep from her cell phone, and Jess fumbled for it and answered. "Shepard."

"Hey, what's up? You sound out of it."

"I fell asleep on the couch last night." Jess yawned. "Why are you calling me so early?"

"Early? Partner, look outside. It's dark."

"What?" Jess leaped up and glanced at her clock. "That can't be!"

"I don't know what happened to you today, but I covered your butt with Tabor."

"Okay. Thanks. I don't know how this could have happened," Jess said, appalled at her lapse. "So what's up?"

Mike's voice took on a note of excitement. "There's been a murder, and we drew the case. I figure the lieutenant wants to find out if you're as hot as everyone says you are."

Was it her imagination, Jess wondered, or did he intend that to have a double meaning? "You almost sound happy."

"Why wouldn't I be? Solving murders is what we do, remember?"

"Right."

"Right. Get your ass to this address now." Mike rattled it off.

"Right. I'm there," Jessica answered and hung up the phone.

She willed herself to get up and get going, but she needed a minute. According to the clock, she'd had more than enough minutes already. An entire day had passed since the last thing she could remember. Jess got up to wash her face and get ready to leave. She looked in the mirror. *A whole day*, she thought. What had happened? She wasn't sure she really wanted to know.

CHAPTER 4

The sky was dark with clouds ripe with imminent rain. The wind off the bay was strong and brought with it a trace of the sea.

Jessica had driven past Pac Bell Park many a time. It was near the water, a serene haven with plenty of grass and stately trees. The kind of place a family would come for a picnic. Or to watch a ball game and binge on hot dogs. The kind of place not normally associated with violent death.

Uniformed officers were holding back the curious. Flashing her badge, Jess ducked under the yellow crime scene tape.

Mike met her halfway to the water's edge and they approached the crime scene together. Partners.

Jess's ex-partner, Wilson Jefferson, broke from the crowd. "Jess! I didn't know they'd called you in on this."

Jess was just as surprised to find him there. She

made the introductions. "Wilson, Delmarco. Delmarco, Wilson."

The two men shook hands and Wilson led the detectives toward the water.

"What do we have?" Jess asked.

Wilson nodded at a strip of shoreline. "It's a floater, male, partially clothed."

Boats from the marine unit had the area cordoned off. "A guy out jogging spotted it and phoned it in. Good thing he did or the next tide might have taken it out."

"Any signs of cause of death?" Mike asked.

Wilson shrugged. "I dunno, man, but on first glance . . . I'd say the guy was beaten to death."

The body lay on its back, arms outstretched. A crime scene photographer was taking stills. A man from the medical examiner's office was there. Officers were taking measurements, searching for clues.

Jess took one look and her stomach churned.

"Jesus!" Mike breathed. "Who did you piss off?"

The victim's face was a pulped, bloody wreck. He had been savagely beaten to the point where he was almost unrecognizable. Almost, but not quite.

Turning away, Jess closed her eyes, thinking over and over, *This can't be happening. This can't be happening.*

Mike misunderstood. "Hey. Listen. Don't worry. You get used to it."

"No, that's not it," Jess said, feeling light-headed.

"Then what?"

Jess forced herself to look at the body. "I think I know him."

Mike and Wilson glanced at one another. "You think?" Mike said.

"Okay. I do know him."

"Shit," Mike said. He stared at the body and then at her. "Shit," he said again. "The lieutenant is going to have a cow." He unclipped his cell phone.

That turned out to be an understatement.

Lieutenant Tabor arrived with Dale Becker in tow. Tabor's clothes were rumpled, as if he had slept in them, and he was smoking cigarettes as if the world were coming to an end and he had to smoke every last one on Earth before it did. He questioned Jess, then left her standing by a squad car and went to talk to the crime scene personnel, and to Delmarco and Wilson Jefferson.

Someone brought Jess a coffee. She sipped it, conscious of the whispers—the whispers and the looks.

Soon Lieutenant Tabor came trudging back, his hands shoved deep in his trench coat. Mike came with him. Becker and several others hung back, eavesdropping.

"So," Tabor said.

"So," Jessica echoed.

"His name is Bob and he drinks gin. There's nothing more you can tell us?" Tabor wore his skepticism on his sleeve.

"I told you. I didn't really know the guy. I met him once, like a month ago."

Tabor wore a pained look. "But you said you were . . ."

"People are intimate all the time," Jess said testily. Becker and several others were giving her funny stares. Mike and Wilson wouldn't meet her gaze.

"With perfect strangers?" Lieutenant Tabor queried. "Hookers are intimate with strangers. That's what they're paid for. Guys hanging out in restrooms at one in the morning are intimate with strangers. Far as I can see, you don't fall into either of those categories. You got another category you want to share?"

"Yes. I picked up a stranger in a bar and had sex with him." Jess said it straight out. "You ever pick up a woman in a bar, Lieutenant?"

"Only in my fantasy life," Tabor said, "the one where God actually likes me." He wearily rubbed his chin. "Okay. I'll put Parker and Lewis on this one."

Mike straightened. "Aw, come on. What is she? A suspect?"

"No. Not at this point. It's just that I doubt Parker or Lewis ever had sex with the guy."

"I can handle it," Jess said. "I swear."

Lieutenant Tabor gave them both searching scrutinies. "Why is it I have this terrible feeling I'll regret this?"

Mike and Jess both relaxed a little, knowing he was about to give in.

"Sometimes I'm too damn nice for my own good," Tabor muttered. "The two of you can remain on the case pending developments that might indicate a conflict of interest."

Jess nodded to Tabor, signaling she understood. The lieutenant walked off and joined Becker and the other officers on the scene.

"Thanks for that," Jessica said to Mike.

"Hey, what are partners for?"

All the photographs had been snapped and all the measurements taken, and now Jess and Mike had the immediate crime scene to themselves.

Delmarco took a step back. "You get first dibs. Let's see what you've got."

Jess went into pure cop mode. She wanted to prove to Mike, to everyone, that her promotion was no fluke. She focused on the shore, and intently surveyed the scene, mentally sorting and arranging all the elements. "Dead less than twenty-four hours."

"How do you know that?" Mike quizzed her.

"The state of the body. The bruises. No decomposition. I could be wrong, but I bet the coroner will bear me out."

"You're not wrong."

She went into overdrive, a homicide computer spewing facts.

"Overkill maybe points to impulse. Hard to tell forethought. Killer is smart. Crime scene is clean, too clean: no tracks, no prints."

Mike just watched her work. "What?" Mike prompted.

"I don't think it was done here."

Mike smiled and nodded in agreement. "Right. Good. So?"

"We oughta check the tide charts. The body might have drifted here on the tide."

"Exactly." Mike gazed out over the bay. "The bay's got two ebb and flow tides each day. This guy could've floated a long way."

"Great. How the hell are we ever going to find where the crime took place?"

Mike held up a key.

"What's that?"

Grinning, Mike stepped to the edge of the water and called out to a sergeant on a nearby police boat, "Hey, Lopez! My key still good?"

Sergeant Lopez was small and wiry and had a pencil mustache. "Your key will always be good, Mike. She'll be waiting for you."

At Jessica's puzzled glance, Mike said, "Marine Unit—my old unit. I used to spend eight to ten hours a day out on the water, with all that sun and fresh air."

"You gave it up to spend half your time behind a desk?"

"Sounds crazy, eh? But boarding boats to look for drugs and contraband just didn't do it for me. I had a great tan, but my brain was turning to mush. I needed more than that. I needed a challenge."

"So what's the key for?"

"Tomorrow, we'll take a little boat ride, you and me."

Jess threw a last glance at the corpse. Her eyes moved over the battered face, the crushed flesh and smashed lips, down over the bruised neck and along one arm. Then she spotted it. On the back of Bob's chalk white hand was a red mark about the size of a pencil eraser, perfectly round, perfectly centered. It couldn't have gotten there by accident. The discovery showed on her face.

"What is it?"

Mike leaned down for a closer look.

"A cigarette burn," Jess said. "Perfectly centered. And it looks fresh."

They exchanged a look.

"Better get a photo," Mike instructed.

Jess found the photographer, who was packing up to go. He remembered taking a shot of the hand, but wasn't sure if it included the burn mark, so he returned with her to take a close-up.

Standing back to watch, Jess stared at the burn. Suddenly, for no apparent reason, one of the photos in her box came to mind, the one with the bloodred X. She shook her head to dispel it, but the image lingered.

Mike had squatted and was inspecting the cuffs of Sherman's pants. He unrolled one and out spilled fine particles of sand.

From over at the ballpark rose the cheers of the crowd. A player had hit a home run and the spectators were going wild.

"Wonder what it's like?" Mike said at Jess's elbow.

"What?"

"A nice, quiet normal life. Working from nine to five and then home every night with the wife and the kids. No corpses, no violence, no lingering questions."

"Are you talking real life or the lieutenant's fantasy world where God loves everyone?"

Mike chuckled. "Real life. I'm told people really can and, in fact, do live that way. Although I'd have to see it to believe it."

"My, my. You're a cynic, Inspector Delmarco."

"And you're not, Inspector Shepard?"

"No, I don't think so. Why do you think so?"

"You don't want to hear it," Mike said.

"Sure I do." Jess was grinning, thinking they were just joking around. But Mike was serious.

"Only a cynic goes for one-night stands."

Jessica's temper flared. "Know that for a fact, do you? I'm sorry. Should I be calling you Mr. Delmarco? How dare you make judgments?"

"I'm a cop. My survival is based on making judgments. And I'm also your partner. So whatever you do is fine by me."

"It was only this once." The words were out of Jess's mouth before she could stop herself.

"Doesn't matter. But what does matter is that I need to know I can find you when I need you. Even if it means interrupting a booty call."

Jess wasn't letting him off so easily. "You say whatever I do is fine. But in the very next breath you judge me for wanting a little sex."

Mike faced her. "Since when is anything about sex 'little'?"

"Are you bragging, Inspector?"

He had to laugh. And that broke the tension that had built between them. Mike shook his head and held out his hands. "Consider the subject closed. Peace?"

Although part of her didn't want to, Jessica shook. "Peace."

They walked toward their cars. Jess dearly wished she could tell him more. Wished she could share the rest so maybe he would understand. But she was deathly afraid of how he would take it.

Mike threw her a look.

"What?"

"I was just thinking that you are many things, partner. But boring isn't one of them."

*　*　*

The bay was glorious in the morning. The warm sun, the spray of water over the bow, the raucous cries of gulls. To Jessica it was a tonic. She had spent the previous night tossing and turning, too overwrought to get much sleep. Now, invigorated by a cup of coffee and the thrill of being out on the high-powered police craft, she smiled with a new-found exuberance. "You gave this up? I think you're the one who should be seeing a shrink."

Mike handled the wheel with the deft skill of an experienced boater. "Maybe so. We all have our secrets."

They were about to pass under the Lefty O'Doul Bridge, the water roiling in their wake. To their left was Pac Bell Park. At the crime scene a few criminologists from CSI were cleaning up the site. Mike waved to one of them and the CSI guy waved back.

"You must know half the department," Jess mentioned.

"A poker buddy."

"Ah. Any other vices I should know about?" Jess asked without thinking and immediately regretted it because it brought Bob Sherman to mind.

"Butterscotch and brandy, not necessarily in that order." Mike opened the throttle a bit more. "Oh. And fishing. My dad taught me when I was a kid, but I rarely get to do it anymore. Never enough time."

Jess thought of all the things her father and

mother had never been able to teach her and felt a dash of envy.

Their boat was ripping across the bay. They passed barges, passed oceangoing vessels, some inbound and some outbound. They passed scores of fishing boats and pleasure craft.

The wind tossed Jess's hair, making a mess of it, but she didn't care. "Any brothers and sisters?"

"Two of each. Both my sisters are older and love to boss me around. Both my brothers are younger, so I get to boss them. You?"

"I was an only child. Didn't have many close friends, either."

"Must have been lonely."

"It was." Sometimes it seemed to Jess that her entire life had been one aching pit of loneliness. From that terrible day when her parents were found dead to now, she had never once been close to anyone. She looked up to find Mike staring at her. "Yes?"

"I've picked up a few girls in bars from time to time. Not that I'm bragging. I just want you to know you're not the only one."

Warmth that had nothing to do with the sun coursed through Jess. "What an uncharacteristically kind thing to say."

"I'm wounded. Deeply. But also incredibly kind and at times incredibly horny."

"Why isn't there a Mrs. Delmarco stashed away somewhere?"

"Probably for the same reason there isn't a Mr. Shepard. We're married to our careers, you and I."

Mike returned his attention to the water, leaving Jess to ponder his words and her choices.

Piers lined the shore, jutting into the bay like accusing fingers. Beyond reared the city proper: Transamerica, Coit Tower, Telegraph Hill. It was a spectacular view, and it gave Jess a whole new appreciation for the beauty of her birthplace.

"Any observations you have, feel free to share," Mike remarked.

"Be easy for someone to dump a body off one of those piers," Jess observed.

"Yeah, it would," he said, unimpressed by her easy solution.

"But . . . we don't think that happened, do we?"

Jess was pretty sure what he *didn't* think happened, but anything else running through Mike's mind was a mystery. He said nothing as he expertly guided the small boat through the waterfront area. The sea lions basking in the sun said more than the enigmatic inspector.

The sight of fishing boats near the shore seemed to jolt him back into cop mode.

"Marine Unit patrols the coast, all up and down the bay," he told Jess. "Looks pretty calm, but not all these guys are just bringing in the catch of the day. San Francisco's always been the preferred port of call for all sorts of smuggling. Any kind of illegal product or person they can float on any size or shape vessel. Heroin. Cocaine. Party drugs. Illegal pharmaceuticals. You name it."

"Didn't I read about a huge bust a couple of years ago? Tons of drugs of all kinds from south of the border?"

"I was in on that," Mike revealed. "An entire yacht had been converted to one giant hold. They would have gotten away with it except they were so weighted down, they were twice as low in the water as they should be. It made me suspicious."

"Was that your biggest bust?"

"Yep. And the one that brought me to Homicide. You're not the only one to ride the coattails of publicity and dumb luck."

Jess gave him a small smile. So it was probably more than just luck of the draw that she had Mike as her partner. She'd never know just what had gone on at headquarters to team them, and right now she didn't care. Mike felt like a good fit.

A long row of pilings swept into view. Spaced closely together, they formed a barrier to the outside world. Under them was an eerie, murky realm where prying eyes couldn't intrude.

Mike cut back on the throttle and angled toward the pilings at a crawl. Shadows fell across them and the temperature seemed to drop a few degrees. With it came a powerful stench reminiscent of rotten eggs.

"Where are you taking me?" Jessica inquired.

"Into the heart of evil."

CHAPTER 5

Something in the way Mike Delmarco said it brought goose bumps to Jessica's skin. She had a sudden premonition that if they floated in among the pilings something terrible would happen, but she told herself it was childish.

"You would be amazed what we find there," Mike was saying. "Hundreds of dump sites, hiding places. I've chased lots of guys under there. None of them ever got away."

"You have X-ray vision?" Jessica joked.

"I know every nook and cranny. Every secret spot," Mike said with a certain pride.

"You're a regular water rat."

"At your service."

They were past the pilings now, abreast of a small house that jutted out over the water. Mike nodded. "See that place?"

"Someone live there?"

Mike gave her what she construed as a sexy look. "Someone very close to you."

"*You* live there?" Somehow Jess had imagined him in a posh condo or ritzy apartment. "Stranger, you're just one big surprise after another."

"You up for a cappuccino?"

Jess glanced at the house, then at him. She had grown comfortable with him, but not quite *that* comfortable.

"Hang on." Mike spun the wheel in a sharp turn.

Nearly knocked off her feet, Jess recovered and clung on. They were speeding past high-masted ships along Pier 23. One was rigging out to get under way.

"Tell me, skipper, just what are we looking for?"

This may have been Mike's home turf, but she was not going to concede the game. She was determined to figure this out before him. It was personal.

Mike was gazing landward. "Something sandy."

"Something sandy? What does that mean?"

"Well, you checked the victim's cuff last night, didn't you?"

Jess thought back and realized she'd missed something. She had to admit it, and if Mike guessed, he didn't let on. "So you saw sand in his cuffs, which tells us he was dragged . . . along a beach."

"Very good, Inspector. If he was, then the drag

marks might still be visible and we might luck out and find a few more clues."

Jessica had been toying with an idea for a while and now she asked, "Mind if I drive?"

" 'Drive?' " Mike said skeptically. "I don't know. This thing's pretty delicate."

Jess grinned. "Aw, gimme a try."

Mike hesitated. That was his mistake. Jess grabbed the controls, shouldering him aside. She gunned the throttle as she had seen him do and he was the one who almost pitched into the drink. The bow rose and the boat took off as if she had popped a wheelie. She laughed for sheer joy. "I could get used to this!"

"Take it real easy," Mike cautioned. "Go slow." He lost his footing. "Hey!"

Another boat came out of nowhere to starboard. Jess frantically spun the wheel to miss it and they cleared it by a hair. The operator of the other craft shook a fist and yelled something she couldn't hear, but which she was sure wasn't flattering. She straightened their boat out just in time to spot another craft to port. "Damn. Where did they come from all of a sudden?"

"Submarines, obviously," Mike cracked.

By accident Jess turned directly into the other boat's wake and they began bouncing up and down in the choppy water. She had to hold on to the wheel tight to keep her footing.

"Okay. You've had enough chances to kill me for one day." Smiling, Mike took over.

Both of them laughed. Jess was feeling more comfortable by the minute. It was great being partners, maybe even great being with him. Abruptly, she spied Alcatraz ahead, and her good mood evaporated. In the distance was the Golden Gate Bridge. It sparked a memory—a memory of the night she was with Bob. Of the beach at Chrissy Field. Of a cluster of trees near the shore. Of Bob Sherman alive and laughing and playfully pulling her toward those trees, and of the feeling of anticipation deep inside her at the prospect of what they were about to do.

"Why did you clam up so suddenly?" Mike wondered. "Don't tell me you're getting seasick."

"Over there," Jess said, pointing at a sandy shore.

Mike noted a strange look on her face, but said nothing. He nodded and slowed and piloted their boat smoothly up onto the beach. Once it came to a stop, he killed the engine and hopped down and hauled a mooring line to a tree and snagged it fast, all with a minimum of wasted movement.

Jess followed him out of the boat and they began their surveillance of the shore.

Mike took only a few steps when he halted and crouched. "Y'know, this looks like the sand could've been brushed clean. See all these tiny lines?" He looked left, then right, then stepped to a fair-size broken tree branch and picked it up. The leaves were still on it. "Fresh off the tree," he said. "And see the sand on the leaves? This could have been what was used."

A pair of joggers came toward them, a young couple with a tiny fluffy dog. The man threw a red ball into the surf and the dog dashed in after it and came back out, soaking wet.

The woman was more interested in them and their boat. "Hi, there. Are you the police?"

"Yes, ma'am," Mike politely answered. "Live around here?"

The pair stopped, but continued running in place. The dog stood with the ball in its mouth, expectantly waiting.

"About a mile away," the man said.

Jess took a turn. "Come here often?"

"Every day," the woman said. "My husband and I are fitness freaks. We wouldn't miss our jog for the world."

"See anything unusual along here yesterday or the day before?" Mike inquired. "Anything at all?"

The husband shook his head. "Not that I remember, no."

"Buffy did go running into the trees at one point," the wife mentioned. "She hardly ever does that. I had to yell and yell before she came back out."

"She was just being her usual stupid self, dear," the man said.

"Cut that out, Artie. You know she understands us. It's not good for Buffy's self-esteem."

"Which trees?" Jess probed.

The woman pointed at the exact cluster where Jess and Bob Sherman had made love.

"Anything else, Officers?" the husband asked. "If we stay here too long our heart rates will go down and we'll have to run an extra quarter mile."

"Work up a sweat," Mike said, and waved them on. He threw the tree branch down. "I guess we should have a look."

Jess's legs were wooden. She moved stiffly among the tangle of branches. Again memories of the night with Sherman surfaced. She held on to the large branches, suspending herself as he moved in under her and hoisted her around his hips. The two of them moving faster and faster and harder and harder until she—

"I doubt anything would've happened over here," Mike declared. "Too risky. Someone would've seen." He pointed inland at where other joggers were moving along a path and some teenagers were smoking cigarettes.

"Maybe not late at night," Jess said.

Mike looked at her. His face was inscrutable. "So what do you think? Anything?"

"Nothing," Jess said.

"Worth calling out the CSI team or wasting their time?" Mike wanted to be absolutely sure of her opinion.

"Wasting it."

"Okay." Mike consulted his wristwatch. "So our morning has been a bust. But maybe the ME will come up with something. Let's roll or we'll be late."

The basement autopsy room was spotless. So clean, a person could eat off the floor. Not that anyone would, Jess reflected. The smell of antiseptic and other odors made her crinkle her nose.

On a slab under a bright overhead light lay the mortal remains of Bob Sherman. Standing beside him was the San Francisco Police Department Medical Examiner, Lisa Banks. Standing next to her was Mike.

Jess did not care to get too close. Every time she looked at Bob's face she flashed back to their tryst, to him inside her and her rhythmic swinging from the tree. Her throat had gone dry, and she swallowed a few times to relieve it.

"So let's hear what you've got," Mike prompted.

"Okeydoke." Lisa touched the corpse. "Bob Sherman, white male, age thirty-two. In reasonably good health at the time he became deceased."

"Reasonably?" Mike said.

"Except for an ingrown toenail and an old appendectomy scar," Lisa clarified. "Now can I finish or would you rather do this yourself?" When Mike sheepishly bowed his head, she resumed. "Confirm death eight to nine hours prior to discovery.

Weapon was a small, blunt object. The kill shot was the blow to the right temple, though he was definitely beaten postmortem as well."

Jess felt as if she had to contribute something so she interjected, "Do you think the killer knew exactly where to hit him?" Not all blows were lethal—most, in fact, were not.

"Hard to say since the victim was hit both before and after death was administered. Most of the beating was postmortem, though. Whoever did this was venting some serious steam."

Jess glanced away.

"Trace evidence," Lisa said. "Nada."

"What do you mean, 'nada'?" Mike asked.

"It's Spanish for 'nothing.'"

Mike muttered something in what sounded like Chinese.

"No fabrics, no hairs. No trace elements whatsoever," Lisa disclosed. "Hell. I even tented the guy. Superglued him up, didn't raise a single latent. That's highly unusual."

"In other words," Mike translated, "whoever did this knew how to cover his or her tracks."

"Extremely well, in my opinion."

"Thanks, Lisa." Mike shook her hand and headed for the door.

Jess was lost in a memory again and didn't realize they were through. She snapped back to action when she heard Mike say, "Shepard!"

"So we're back to square one, aren't we?" Jess said, covering.

"We never left it," Mike said.

The next morning, Jess and Mike waited their turn to report on their case. Dale Becker was just finishing the details of his case.

"Anyway, the ex confessed after we shook him a little."

"Great." The lieutenant shifted. "Delmarco? Shepard? Where are you guys on yours?"

Mike broke it down for him: their search of the bay, their visit to the ME's office, concluding with "The crime scene was clean. No weapon, no prints, no witnesses."

"And no suspect," Lieutenant Tabor said. He wasn't pleased.

"We're going out to neighbors and known acquaintances today," Jess said, to show they weren't twiddling their thumbs.

"Anything else?" Tabor asked.

"Actually, yeah." Jess sat up. "I'd like to put out the word to stay on the lookout for similar vics coming in. Males, twenty to thirty, severely beaten."

Dale Becker snorted. "Wait a second. You got one body and you're already thinking serial? What is this, spotlight withdrawal?"

Some of the other detectives laughed. Jess felt herself grow hot, but restrained herself.

Even Lieutenant Tabor was grinning. "Here's some advice I like to share with new inspectors." He was being condescending. "It's sort of like Homicide AA. One body at a time. Okay?"

"Yes, sir," Jessica said.

"Good. Back to work. If anyone needs me, I'll be in my office waging combat with my ulcer."

There was more laughter. Mike stood and beckoned and Jess followed him to the coffee room and on to the lobby. She ripped open multiple packets of sugar she'd stuffed into her pocket and mixed them into her cup.

"What? I like sugar . . ."

"I was just wondering. Do I get let in on this, or what? I mean, it's sort of traditional for partners to confide in each other."

"Sorry. I put you on the spot up there, didn't I?" Mike shrugged.

"It's just that the cigarette burn reminded me of this case I read about," Jess said. "It's just a hunch, whatever. It's stupid, obviously. . . ."

"You never know." Mike gave her a level stare. "If it's stupid like the hunch that led to Culter, why don't you bring it on? Partner, I got your back."

"Thanks, Mike," Jess said. Their eyes met, but she was bothered by a troubling thought he had sparked: *What if they found out the truth about her hunch?*

*   *   *

Holding cells were always small. Jess stared in at Eddy Culter, amazed by the transformation. His hair had been trimmed and combed, his face shaved. Gone was the beast. In its place was an earnest, seemingly normal, seemingly sincere young man. He had a bandage on his nose.

Culter glanced at her, then said to his attorney, "Ask her. She knows what she did."

"If you don't want to talk to her, you don't have to," Ray Porter said. His suit was the best his extremely large bank account could buy. As one of San Francisco's top twenty most eligible bachelors, he dressed the part and was fond of silk shirts monogrammed with his initials.

Culter had his story down pat. And his poor, put-upon innocent routine. "She picked me up and lured me to that place. She got rough. I mean, I had no idea she was an officer, Mr. Porter."

Porter just nodded. His client was giving an award-winning performance. He would do just fine in court.

"Wouldn't you say that was entrapment, sir? And then she kicked me in the face while I was down. Isn't there a law against police brutality?"

Ray frowned. "That's enough, Edmund," he cautioned.

Then Culter sounded even more pathetic. If that were possible, Jess thought.

"I've been going through all this pain and suffering, Mr. Porter."

"Well, I'm sorry about that, Edmund. Now that I'm on the case, we'll certainly be petitioning the judge to reconsider your bail. We'll be pursuing many other options. You're going to be fine."

Culter had the smile of an innocent choirboy. That would play well in court, too.

Jess stood at the door as Porter and Culter left the cell. Still looking the victim, Culter hissed as he passed her, "I know your little dirty side, lady. I know you. You're *me*."

Too stunned to reply, Jess was glad the bailiff hauled him off before she hit him again. She stood facing Ray Porter. "Ray, please tell me you're not gonna represent this loser."

"That loser's daddy is Culter Pharmaceuticals. We golf together Tuesdays at the Olympic Club. He's asked me to defend his boy as a favor."

"Favor, hell. You're doing it for the money. You always do it for the money."

Porter smiled. She was sharp.

Mike finished his conversation with one of the guards and joined them in time to hear Jess let Porter know what she thought.

"Aw, Ray, when you were assistant DA, you used to nail bad guys' asses to the wall like trophies."

"Yeah, Porter," Mike threw in. "Whatever happened to crime doesn't pay?"

"Gee, Delmarco," Ray said blandly, "I don't know. Whatever happened to innocent until proven guilty? Cops never make mistakes? *You* ever make a mistake, Delmarco?"

Jess realized the two had a history. A bitter history, based on Porter's attitude.

"Never," Mike said.

"You know what I'm talking about," Ray said enigmatically. He took hold of Jess's arm. "Would you excuse us? I'd like to talk to Jessica for a minute in private, please."

Jess nodded to Mike and he moved off, his jaw muscles clenching.

Jess let Ray Porter pull her a few feet; then she pulled her arm free from his grasp. "What do you want?"

"This guy, Delmarco. He tends to go off the deep end. Be careful."

"*Mike* tends to go off the deep end?" Jess rebutted. "Ray, you've got a client with a whole string of murders in his past."

"Every defendant has the right to his day in court. Young man's got no prior convictions."

"Come on, Ray," Jess said. "He's the guy. I nabbed him in the act."

Porter's lips curved suggestively. "Sometimes, nabbing the bad guy is the easy part."

"Yeah? And what's the hard part?" Jess could feel her anger building.

"The hard part is learning how to relax," Ray said. "Jess, Homicide investigators have got to testify in court all the time. Your testimony will be more effective and more believable if you're relaxed. So you have to relax and maybe you need someone to help you with that." He stepped closer.

"Stop it."

Ray bent down so only she would hear. "I think about that night. I think about it a lot. Always thought you'd come back, but you never did."

"I told you I wouldn't," Jess said coldly. "It was one night and one night only." *Just like all the rest,* she thought.

Ray stepped back, seemingly unperturbed by the rebuff. "Hey, you gotta come see my new place."

Jess glanced over Ray's shoulder and saw Mike watching them.

"Here." Porter fished in a pocket and flourished a business card emblazoned with the same stylized initials that monogrammed his shirt. "This has my new address and my new phone number. The private one. You give me a call if you need me. For anything. I'm there for you."

Don't get me. Don't get anything. Some guys just don't get it, she thought. She shook her head and turned away from Ray Porter. She heard his parting words as she started to leave.

"Don't hate me, Jessica. It's *not me*. It's the *process*."

CHAPTER 6

John Mills's house was big and solid brick, like the commissioner himself. His rooftop deck boasted a barbecue grill and a magnificent view of the city by the bay. Under the late-afternoon sun, he was relating the latest gossip while flipping steaks and checking baked potatoes by pricking the aluminum foil with a fork.

"So North Side thinks they've got a perv case on their hands because of the bite marks on the body. Only no one bothers to find out whether the guy's got a dog . . . what?"

One look, and he knew Jess had something on her mind.

"Ray Porter's defending Culter."

Mills poked a potato. "I teach him the ins and outs, and now he's walking the other side of the street. There's a lesson for me. Gotta be more careful who you train." He raised a steak high enough to check the bottom. "So what's he arguing? That this piece of shit Culter didn't do it?"

"I don't know," Jess said, even though she had a pretty good idea exactly how Porter would attack her credibility. "I kicked the guy."

"That you did, Inspector Shepard, that you did." Mills smiled. "The lousy skell goes around grabbing girls and sticking a knife into them. He deserved a piece of your mind."

Jess didn't tell him there was more to her bust. A whole lot more. And if it came out in court, she would be exposed. "I'm glad you see it my way."

"How else would I see it?" Mills placed a steak and a potato on a plate and set the plate in front of her. "Dig in. Medium rare, as you like."

"I can't believe you never married. You're such a fine cook." Jess sliced off a piece and slowly chewed, savoring the taste.

"Did you ever think I didn't tie the knot because I became too used to batching it?" Mills sat across from her. "We get used to things a certain way and that's how we always want them."

Jess said half to herself, "I wish I could change."

"Why? You're down on yourself over Culter? Sure, Porter will claim the guy was cuffed and all that civil rights bullshit, and blah, blah, blah. But in the end, it's your word against his." He forked steak into his mouth. "He was resisting. Remember that. That's your story and you stick to it." He wagged his steak knife at her. "Don't make it fancy.

Don't get creative. Just stick to your story. You'll be fine."

"Thanks for the advice."

"What else are mentors for?" Mills was a paragon of reassurance. "Hell, everything's fine. And what's not fine can be fixed. And for what can't be fixed, there's Zinfandel." He checked the label of the wine bottle, then filled her long-stemmed glass.

"So. How's your case going?"

"Don't worry. I'm all over it," Jess lied yet again.

"That's my girl," John Mills said.

The ceiling in Dr. Frank's office had a crack Jess hadn't noticed before, leading her to reflect that she and the ceiling had more in common than anyone would ever guess.

"Go on," Dr. Frank urged. "You were saying?"

"They called it the Golden Gate case. Five male victims, all marked with red X's. Then he shot my mother. And then he shot himself."

"I've seen some of the news stories," Frank said.

Jess had them all. Every last clipping from every last newspaper, all stored in the box in her closet. "Anyway, my father's partner took me in, took care of me." She looked at the psychiatrist. "You know how cops are. They treat each other's families like their own. Lucky for me."

"I'm not sure I'd call you lucky. Being the daughter of a murder victim and a serial killer."

"I don't really think about it that way," Jessica said defensively.

"Oh. What way do you think about it?"

"I think of myself as a cop. Period. End of story."

"So as a cop then. How are things?"

"Fine." Jess glared at him as she answered. "The case is going great . . . except that we have no suspects."

"And does that make you angry?" Dr. Frank pressed.

Jess sighed. "Here we go again."

"Resist all you want, but it will only mean more sessions. Until you confront yourself you'll never be able to overcome your anger or any other emotional problems you might have."

Every muscle in Jess's body grew rigid. "Now you think I have other problems? The list keeps growing and growing."

Dr. Frank wouldn't let it drop. "*Do* you have any problems you haven't told me about? Secrets you're keeping to yourself."

"I told you I would be honest with you, didn't I? The least you can do is trust me, for God's sake."

"You have that backwards, Inspector Shepard," Frank said. "I'm the one you should trust. But you don't. You're hiding something from me. Every professional instinct I have tells me so."

"Instincts can be wrong."

"Okay. Keep playacting. Keep hoping I'll tire of all this cat and mouse and end your therapy so you can get on with your life." Dr. Frank scribbled on his clipboard. "But that's not going to happen. I take my responsibilities seriously."

"Lucky me, huh?" Jess said. Inside she was scared, more scared than she had ever been, scared that her whole life would come crashing down around her if he delved too deep. She had to do something.

The only thing was, she didn't know what.

Jessica's shift was almost over. She was typing a report, anxious to get it done and have some downtime.

Over at the window, Mike Delmarco fiddled with the venetian blinds. "All our work and we turn up zip."

"We'll visit more of Sherman's friends tomorrow," Jess proposed. "Someone is bound to know something."

"I've got it," Mike said, trying to make light of the hours they had spent fruitlessly pounding the pavement. "The butler did it. With a rope in the pantry."

Dale Becker was listening from across the room. "Gee, what's it been? Five days? And you're no closer now to solving it than you were when you first saw the body?"

"Did I ask for your input?" Jess snapped.

"I'm offering it free. Such as this gem. Did you know that after the first twenty-four hours, if you don't have a suspect, the chances of solving the crime drop exponentially?"

"Did you know that if you spend the first thirty years of your life as an asshole, the chances of your ever not being one drop exponentially?" Jess gave him a dose of his own sarcasm.

There was laughter, and Dale fingered his stapler as if debating whether to throw it at her.

"Children, please." Lieutenant Tabor had approached unnoticed. "Make nice or I'll move your sandboxes farther apart."

"That would suit me, sir," Dale said.

"What's your beef, Inspector Becker? Is it that Inspector Shepard is female? Is it that she's new to Homicide? All of the above?"

"I've worked with female officers before and had no complaints, sir," Dale responded. "And everyone is new and green at one point."

"Then what?" Tabor persisted.

"I think her being here is a fluke, Lieutenant. I think dumb luck is all she has going for her, and that's not enough."

There was that word again, Jess reflected: *luck*.

Lieutenant Tabor was in a fence-mending mood. "Cut her some slack, Dale. She hasn't been here a whole week yet. Give her a chance to prove herself. The same chance I once gave you."

"Is that an order, sir?"

"Unequivocally. I can carve it into your forehead if that will help you remember," Tabor said. At that,

Dale Becker got up in disgust and left. Tabor lightly rapped his knuckles on Jess's desktop. "Don't make me eat my words, Shepard. And don't mind Becker too much. He's headstrong, but he's good at his job. A trait I believe you two share." He smiled and headed for his office.

Mike had been quiet during the whole exchange. Now he came up behind her and leaned over her chair. "Are you about done there, partner?"

"Another minute. Why?"

"I'd like to treat you to a drink at La Bodega."

Jess's fingers turned to stone. "That's where I made Culter." She couldn't fathom why Mike wanted to go there, of all places. "Any special reason?"

"I'd like to see it for myself. Find out why you chose to stake it out. Get a better idea of how your mind works."

Night had fallen by the time they arrived. The parking lot was full, as always, the place hopping. Mike wanted to sit near the front, where the flamenco dancer was tapping a sensual cadence, but Jess steered him to a corner table in the shadows. A waiter came and brought them sangria.

Jess pulled a cigarette out, but didn't light it. She rolled it from one finger to the next, a release for her overwrought nerves. Mike was prattling on about something, but she wasn't really paying much attention.

She mindlessly watched the dancer, and suddenly blurted, "Castanets!"

Mike got the reference immediately: name a homicide involving castanets. "Hmm."

He had to think about this one. Jess was sure she had him.

"Toledo, Ohio. Nineteen eight-two. A young male flamenco dancer was found murdered with the imprints of a castanet upon his throat."

He'd done it. "Bartender! More sangria!" Jess called. She never would have thought anyone could be murdered with castanets. Then again, she never thought like a murderer. But chances were, neither did her father at first. She shook off the possibility and the memory. She was going to enjoy herself.

Then she gazed toward the entrance and one of her past mistakes.

Jimmy Schmidt had just walked in. He was in civvies, so he was off duty. He spotted her the same instant she spotted him, and leered.

Mike was too observant for her own good. "There's your boyfriend."

"He's not. He's an ex," Jess said. "He's also the reason I don't get, you know, overly friendly with my coworkers anymore."

"Good to know." Delmarco smiled and waved, but Jimmy didn't wave back. "He doesn't seem to like me much."

"He doesn't like anybody much except himself."

Mike gave Jimmy one last look and got back to

business. "So how did this Culter thing happen again? What was this guy's trigger?"

"The place . . . it was the only place with a view of all three crime scenes."

"So you started hanging out there after work, waiting on him?" Mike looked around again. "Boy, you musta really wanted to make inspector."

"Didn't you?"

"More than anything," Mike confessed, and abruptly switched topics. "They made you do the shrink thing, right? I mean, they usually do when you pop a guy."

Jess figured it was a coincidence, but it unnerved her. "Yeah. Makes you feel like you screwed up."

"Sounds to me like you did all right."

The flamenco dancer was building to her grand finale. Her red shoes were striking the floor like pistons, her dress constantly swirling this way and that, her fingers clicking the castanets to the frenzied tempo of her dance.

Jess knew Jimmy Schmidt was staring at her, but she refused to so much as acknowledge his existence. She hoped he wouldn't make a scene, but she should have known better. The moment the dance ended and the customers were applauding, a shadow fell across their table.

"I thought you might be here. I've been coming every night for a week." Jimmy glared at Delmarco. "Didn't expect to find you slumming."

"Inspector Mike Delmarco, meet Patrol Officer Jimmy Schmidt."

Jimmy never knew when to leave well enough alone. "Inspector, huh? Is this your new partner, babe? Going to get all cozy with him like you did with me?"

"Go to hell, Jimmy," Jessica said.

"What? Now I'm garbage? That wasn't how you acted that night we were together. What say you ditch him and the two of us go someplace we can be alone?"

Jess had half a notion to fling her wine in his face. "What say we don't and just pretend we did? Leave, Jimmy. And don't bother me again."

Schmidt grasped her wrist. "Come on. You know you want to just as much as I do. My car is right outside."

"The lady has made it plain she doesn't want to go." Mike rose. "I suggest you take your hand off her."

"Or what?" Jimmy growled. "You'll take me out back and kick my ass? That'll be the day."

"Or you'll find yourself explaining to your captain why you were forcing your attentions on a fellow officer," Mike said calmly.

Jimmy made a show of slowly removing his hand and stepping back. "By the book, huh? Fine. See you babe," he said to Jess, and stalked off.

Mike shook his head. "You sure can pick them."

A sharp retort was on the tip of Jess's tongue, but

she held it in. He was only making small talk, not accusing her of anything. "Let's just say I haven't had the best of luck where men are concerned." And there was that word again: *luck.*

"Maybe, and this is just a suggestion, mind you, but maybe you need to be more choosy about who you drink with, or whatever."

"Including you?" she shot back. It shut him up. At least for the moment.

Jess downed more wine and ordered a refill. The lively mood of the crowd was infectious and it wasn't long before she had forgotten about Jimmy Schmidt and Eddy Culter and Bob Sherman and the rest, and was enjoying herself again. Mike appeared to be having a good time, too, and he related his childhood on the mean streets of Los Angeles, and told her about how his family moved to San Francisco when he was twelve.

Jess liked to hear him talk. He had a nice voice and a real nice body and a face that most women would give a second glance. The hours passed so quickly that when he mentioned the place was getting ready to close, she was shocked.

Outside, a stiff breeze stirred the trees. North Beach had yet to wind down. Groups of friends were emerging from bars. Couples lingered in front of restaurants or cuddled in doorways.

"I guess this is where we part company until to-morrow," Mike said.

"I guess."

"Tell me something first. And be honest. When you were alone with Culter, did you ever think how maybe it wouldn't be such a bad thing if your gun went off accidentally?"

The startled look on Jess's face was enough for him to back off.

"Sorry. It's just guys like that make my skin crawl, you know?"

Jess saw that he was peering intently back into La Bodega. She turned, thinking he might be watching the flamenco dancer, but he was staring at Jimmy Schmidt, who was showing the dancer his own version of flamenco.

"Yeah," Jess answered, watching Mike watch Jimmy. "I know. Ever since I arrested him, I can't shake the feeling he's still sort of around me. Watching me."

Mike turned his attention back to Jess and really sounded like he meant it as he said, "Well, if I see him, I'll kick his ass for ya."

"Good to know." Jess smiled.

Later, when Jess was alone in her apartment, she thought of the questions Delmarco had asked. Of the roller-coaster vibes the man gave off, one second so helpful and supportive, the next a grand inquisitor.

Seated on her bed, her back propped against a pillow, Jess sipped from a bottle of water and gazed up through the skylight. "What exactly are you,

Michael Delmarco?" she said out loud. "Why do you keep giving off mixed signals?"

She had slipped into a tank top and jeans and was feeling cozy and comfortable. No urge tonight to go out, no carnal craving that couldn't be denied. She would catch up on her sleep and be ready to rock come morning.

Jess thought about Ray Porter and her cozy feeling vanished. He would attack her credibility on the witness stand. She was sure of it. Knowing what he did, he could hit her where it would hurt her reputation the most, and in the process bring her whole house of cards tumbling down.

A faint clicking reached her ears. Jess glanced sharply toward the window. It was closed and locked, exactly as she had left it. The clicking continued but only for a few seconds. She wasn't certain it was the same sound as the night before. It might be something else entirely.

As tired as she was, Jess had no desire to get up and look. She sank further into her pillow and languidly stretched. Moments like this were all too rare in her life and she wasn't moving for anything short of the end of the world.

Then Jess caught movement out of the corner of her eye, or thought she did, and she twisted her head to the right. She strained her eyes into the shadows, but saw nothing to account for it. Everything was as it should be.

She had half a mind to get up and give her apart-

ment a quick check anyway, but her body had
grown woozy, her blood sluggish in her veins. She
rose onto her elbows, but couldn't rise any higher.
The world was blurring. The shadows had come to
life and were crawling toward the bed. Toward her.
Dark fingers reached out for her, and although she
tried with all her mental might to stay awake, she
was swallowed into an inky void.

A jarring ring shattered the emptiness.

Jess felt herself swimming upward from the bottom of a well toward a high, distant light. She
stroked and stroked, but came no closer. Suddenly,
another ring catapulted her toward the light at
breakneck speed. She burst out of the dark into the
world of the living and sat bolt upright, confused
and disoriented.

Her cell phone was insistently demanding it be
answered. Slowly, stiffly, her senses muddled, Jess
fumbled for it and said groggily, "Hello?"

"Jessica!" Delmarco sounded excited.

"What time is it? Did I oversleep again?"

"No." Mike paused. "Mount up! We've got another one!"

"Another one?" Jess asked, trying desperately to
compose herself.

"Our killer has struck again."

CHAPTER 7

Jessica willed her feet toward her mirror. She had to change, brush her hair, and meet Mike downstairs in five minutes. He was already on his way and had phoned en route. Her face was pale. She touched her cheek and wondered if she were coming down with something, a cold or the flu maybe. When she removed her hand, her cheek was streaked scarlet.

Blood was on her fingertips. Bewildered, Jess wiped them on her shirt and examined her fingers to find the cut that caused the bleeding. But there was none. Her skin was unbroken. She examined her cheek in the mirror, but it was fine, too. That meant the blood wasn't hers.

Suddenly light-headed, Jess turned. Everything was exactly as it should be, as it had been when she hopped into bed the night before. There was no one else there, nothing at all to account for it.

"What is happening to me?"

Jess didn't have time to dwell on the mystery, not with Mike due any minute. She quickly changed and readied herself and was out front at the curb when Mike came screeching around the corner and braked with a squeal.

"Hop in. They're waiting for us at the scene."

Jess couldn't get over how pumped he was. "So this is what it takes to start your day with a bang?" she remarked as she fastened her seat belt.

Mike peeled out and hung a sharp right at the intersection. "I told you. I live for this stuff." He spun the steering wheel to avoid a slow-moving truck. "Bridge patrol got another floater."

Jess listened quietly as he ran down the details. "Male, late twenties. And to quote the Marine officer who contacted me, 'Someone pounded the shit out of him.'" When she didn't respond, Mike glanced at her. "Hey, talkin' to ya. You okay?"

"Yeah, okay, fine," Jess said, although she didn't feel fine. She was confused, terribly confused, and more than a little scared.

"Want to stop for some coffee on the way?"

"No, no. They're expecting us." Jess stared toward the Bay Bridge. "How much did we drink last night?"

"Maybe you oughta go easy on that sangria."

"I said I was okay," Jess insisted, peeved at the suggestion she couldn't hold her alcohol.

"That's the attitude I'm looking for," Mike said, and laughed.

His humor was grating, but only because Jess wasn't in the mood to appreciate it. They didn't say much the rest of the way, and when they arrived, he asked again if she was all right. "Ask me again and I'll throw you off the damn bridge," she groused.

CSI was swarming over the decrepit pier. Down below was the Underwater Recovery Team, their boats bobbing in the water. The winch boat was moving into position for the retrieval.

Patrolmen were keeping back the inevitable curious passersby: joggers, walkers, a couple of kids holding skateboards.

Mike approached several officers, whose backs were to him, and said cheerfully, "Hey, one of you patrol guys wanna rustle up some breakfast? Eggs, bacon, toast, that kinda thing, seeing as you're not busy."

One of the patrolmen turned. It was Jimmy Schmidt. "Go to hell, Delmarco."

The unspoken war between Jimmy and Mike continued. Mike, still smiling although his eyes glittered like twin daggers, taunted, "Make that bacon crispy."

Jess concentrated on the activity in the water. Here, amid the pilings, the light was filtered and subdued. The victim was naked, the body snarled in an old fishing net and crisscrossed with clinging seaweed. The face, what little was left of it, gaped blankly into the air.

"Looks like death by blunt-force trauma," she reasoned. "Serious overkill. The vic is male, maybe late twenties."

Two Underwater Recovery men had secured straps under the victim's arms and were hoisting the body up.

Jessica slipped on her gloves and snagged one of the victim's hands. She held it so Mike could see the burn mark—an exact duplicate of the one they had found on Bob Sherman.

Mike nodded. "There's our confirmation."

"Yup, our guy. Looks like he's getting angrier," she answered, "which hopefully means sloppier, too."

Jess looked forward to rubbing Dale Becker's nose in it. He had it coming after how he had treated her.

"What's that on his other hand?" Mike asked.

The Recovery team was hoisting the body higher. As it rose, it turned. Jess saw a mark of some kind. Not a burn, but what appeared to be a tattoo. She reached for the wrist and rotated it so she could see the tattoo clearly.

For a few seconds, the sky and the ground switched places and Jess feared her legs would give out. The tattoo was of a large musical note. She flashed back to the Saloon and the night she had picked up Larry. Jerking back, she wheeled.

"Are you all right?" Mike asked.

"Little queasy," Jess said, which was true enough. She was on the verge of shock. First Bob Sherman, now Larry. *What in God's name is happening?*

Mike put a hand on her shoulder. "I keep forgetting you're new at this. It takes some getting used to."

Although the body had no ID and they wouldn't have fingerprints for a while, Mike made the victim quickly, thanks to the tattoo. He called in a description and the computer spat back a possible. A patrol cop gave him the news.

"We got him. Guy was in the system. Lawrence Geber. Date of birth: twelve eleven sixty-eight. Had a couple of DUIs a while back."

Jess hadn't heard another car drive up. She wasn't paying much attention to the goings-on around her. That heightened her surprise when she heard Lieutenant Tabor's voice right behind her.

"Is that a fact? Not that it will do us much good."

Tabor wasn't alone. With him were Dale Becker and Becker's partner, Sims. All three stared at Jess as if expecting her to say something. Her fear rose. *They must know,* she reasoned. Somehow or other they had found out she slept with Larry, too.

"How did you know?" Lieutenant Tabor demanded.

"Pardon?" Jess said.

"How did you know there'd be another body? And please don't say, 'woman's intuition,' because I'm all maxed out on that front."

Jess's relief was boundless. "Well. There was a cigarette burn on the back of his hand." She stopped, awash in images of Bob and her and then of Larry and her, the images blending into a jumbled riot of sensation.

Mike jumped in, saying, "It's not a simple homicide. The burn was obviously intentional. A signature."

"I'm impressed, Shepard," Lieutenant Tabor said. "You're as good as everyone says you are."

Dale Becker was fit to be tied. Nudging Sims, he walked off.

"I can't say I'm happy you were right. But it was a good call, Shepard," Tabor said. "If the press gets wind of this, we'll have banner headlines making us out to be dunces because we can't solve the case fast enough to suit them. It never fails."

"We'll do our best," Mike promised.

"Okay. Get on this fast. I want this guy stopped before the bodies pile up."

"Yes, sir," Mike said.

Jess realized the lieutenant was looking at her. "Yes, sir," she parroted, and Tabor nodded and moved toward the pilings.

The moment they were alone, Mike whispered, "What's up with you? Why are you acting like a zombie? I know you're tougher than this."

"Think so, do you? How well do you really know me, Inspector Delmarco? Maybe I fall apart every time I see a drop of blood."

"Whoa, there. I'm on your side, remember?"

"Are you?" Jess had no proof of that. She didn't know anything anymore. Her world was crumbling down around her and she didn't have the slightest idea why or the slightest clue who was behind it.

Seeing the bodies separately was bad enough. Seeing them side by side on slabs at the morgue almost made Jess sick. She couldn't bear to look at them. To remember their lips on hers. Their fingers on her body.

Lisa Banks, wearing a pair of orange goggles, was inspecting Larry's body with a handheld UV unit. "This guy thinks he's a pro. This guy thinks he's being real careful about covering his tracks. Not with me, baby. Everybody leaves something behind."

Mike was at her elbow. "I hope you're right."

"I'm always right," Lisa said. "Hold it. What's this?" She bent lower, gave the light and the goggles to her assistant, and slid a magnifying glass from a pocket.

"Sherlock Holmes would be proud," Mike said.

"Don't knock the basics, Inspector," the ME said. "You'd be surprised at how much you find." She aligned the magnifying glass. "Is this what I think it is?" Banks was talking to herself, not to them. "Just give me a little speck of blood. Just one little drop."

Despite her revulsion, Jess leaned forward when the others did and saw the same thing they did: a tiny drop of blood in Larry's hair, behind the right ear.

Banks was doing her version of a victory dance. "Oh yeah! Oh yeah! Like this little drop, for example."

"Is she always like this?" Mike asked the assistant.

"This is one of her saner moments."

Lisa sobered and explained, "You see, the blood spatter on the front of the body matches the angles of the blows." She backed up for everyone to see. "So you tell me what's this drop of blood doing way up here *behind* the ear? It's making my job fun." She passed a swab with the blood to her assistant.

Jess thought about what Lisa had just said. "The blood," she said, "could be the killer's."

"Sherlock Holmes would be proud." Lisa stared down at Mike. "I'm beginning to think there was a Shirley Holmes who solved all the crimes and let Sherlock take the credit. But back to this poor schlub. Maybe he fought back. Maybe this drop of blood isn't his, but the perpetrator's."

Mike got back in the game. "How soon will you know?"

"I've yet to meet a patient detective," Lisa said.

Jess was thinking of the blood on her finger and cheek that morning. "The blood might not be the killer's."

Everyone looked at her as if she had thrown a damper on their party.

"Well," Lisa Banks said, "I have to extract for DNA. I've got to amp it and I've got to type it. That will tell us with absolute certainty whether or not the drop matches the victim's blood. If it doesn't match, I'll run the profile through the felon database. Maybe we'll get lucky."

"When's the soonest?" from Mike.

"For you, Mike, a couple of days. Maybe."

Mike was exuberant on their way back to his car. "We solve this quickly, think of what it will mean when promotion time rolls around."

"It's just one case," Jess reminded him.

"This from the person who was promoted to Homicide on the basis of one bust? One case can make all the difference, careerwise. The higher-ups remember the big ones."

"Do I detect a note of raw ambition?"

Mike twirled the ring to his car keys. "Are you going to tell me you don't have any ambition?"

Jess had honestly never given it a lot of thought. She took it for granted she would rise through the ranks. Especially with John Mills rooting for her every rung of the climb. "What will be will be."

"All right then, Doris Day," Mike taunted, "let's get it on."

Before she could "get it on" again, she had one stop to make.

Jess listened to the scratch of pen on paper as Dr. Frank scribbled notes. "Are we finally done?"

"You should be so lucky." Frank slid his glasses to the end of his nose. "You know the hardest thing for a cop to do is to reach out for help because we aren't supposed to need it. We are the help. And if I may say so, you look a little rough around the edges."

"How many times must I tell you I'm fine?"

"Says you. But in my completely objective opinion, you look a little washed-out today. And you're not leaving until you tell me why."

Jess tried a grin. "Oh, I get it. No more Mr. Nice Guy?"

"I think we know each other well enough to skip the small talk," Dr. Frank said. "I want to talk about the F word."

"Excuse me!"

"Feelings. Feelings of being overwhelmed. Feelings of helplessness."

Jess hedged. "I won't talk about my personal life."

"And I wouldn't ask you to. I'm interested in your feelings with regard to your work."

"I've been a little stressed," she admitted. She wasn't ready to admit more than that to anyone—including herself.

"A little?"

"I can't be any more definite than that."

Dr. Frank had her file on his lap, and opened it. "At one point you suffered from stress-related symptoms. Some minor bouts of depression, and—"

Jess raised her head. "Hold it. Are you talking about when I was six? My parents had just died. I was a little sad and didn't know how to handle it."

"Fair enough," Dr. Frank said. "But patterns we pick up early in life tend to linger later on. How do you handle it now?"

"Like most any adult."

"Come on, Jess." It was the first time Frank used her first name. "You can say it." He tapped his head. "The vault, remember? It goes no further than this room."

Jess didn't say anything.

"You know, the stuff we've been talking about, your parents, your childhood, all this could be stirring up a lot—"

"It's not that," Jess interrupted.

"Well, it's . . . ?"

Indecision knifed through her. Jess wanted to tell someone, but she was deathly afraid of doing so. Afraid of the potential repercussions. "It goes no further? No matter what I say?"

"Unless you've committed a crime or are planning to commit a crime, remember?"

"This is so stupid. I have one-night stands."

There. Jess had blurted it out. She looked at him but his face was hard to read.

"What about them?"

"I have a lot, I guess. More than I thought, anyway."

Dr. Frank was as analytical as ever. "Why do you think that is?"

"Because I like sex." Already Jess regretted bringing it up. "Is there something wrong with that? Don't you like sex, Dr. Frank?"

"Yeah, sure. But this isn't about me."

"Yeah, well, you're not a female cop." Jess balled her fists. "We're all supposed to do the same job, but be nuns or virgins on the side. I mean, I started wearing perfume a few months ago and you would have thought I showed up for work in my damn pink tutu."

"You own a pink tutu?"

"This is your idea of therapy?" Jess bristled. "Mocking me?"

"I'm sorry. You brought the tutu up."

"I brought it up because I'm working on my first case and it looks like it's going to be a really big case, and it turns out both the victims are guys I slept with."

Dr. Frank had a strange look. "Both of them?"

Jess sighed. "That's why I brought it up. You know, for someone who is supposed to be able to understand people, you're a little slow on the up-take. What a lousy coincidence, right? On my very first case." Jess had to laugh at the absurdity of it all.

"Now who is being slow?" Dr. Frank asked.

"What?"

"Did you tell your partner about this?"

Swinging her feet to the floor, Jess responded, "Did you not hear that whole nun-virgin speech just now? It's okay for male cops to go around banging bedmates right and left, but let a female cop do it, and she's ruined."

"There's more at stake here."

"What *are* you talking about?"

Dr. Frank had never been more earnest. "Jessica, listen to me. You have to tell your partner. Or your lieutenant. Or someone in the department. You have to tell someone. *You*, not me. I can't. Remember?"

"And have them treat me like a slut?"

Dr. Frank slid to the edge of his chair. "What if it isn't a coincidence? What if you're in danger."

"Me?" Jessica said, stunned by the implication.

"Now who is being slow on the uptake, Inspector Shepard? Yes, you could be in great danger."

CHAPTER 8

It had honestly never occurred to her, but as Jess took the elevator down, it was all she could think about. Bob Sherman's murder was bizarre enough, but Larry, too? She had been with both of them not long before their deaths. Clearly and conclusively, there was a link. How stupid could she be? she asked herself. Or was she in denial, as Dr. Frank kept trying to claim. After all, she had experienced a blackout the night before each body had been found. Presumably, the very nights the two were slain. A case could be made that *she* was to blame.

Badly shaken, Jess recalled the blood on her fingers. Was it Larry's? If so, that put her at the crime scene. But how could she have done something so hideous and not have a recollection of it? Was it some unusual form of sleepwalking? She'd heard about a case where a man was alleged to have murdered his wife in his sleep. Could she have done the same thing? So many questions, so many conflicting answers. They tore at her insides, ravaging her emotionally.

Jess wanted to go home and crawl under the covers and not come out for a week. She needed time to think, to work things out, but it was time she didn't have. Dr. Frank had been right. She must tell someone, and soon. The longer she put it off, the more suspicion would be cast in her direction.

Suddenly, Jess was aware of someone near her car. Her senses sharpened. He was in his mid- to late twenties with stubble sprinkling his chin. He wore an ankle-length coat that could easily conceal a weapon. At the moment he was lighting a cigarette. She was tempted to call out, to demand to know what he was doing next to her car, but she bit off the yell. He might have climbed from any of a dozen other vehicles and was only going about his own business.

The man turned and came toward her. Instinctively, Jess slid her hand under her jacket and unsnapped her Beretta. She had practiced drawing and firing so many times that she could have it out in the blink of an eye. But up close she would be vulnerable, and the stranger was coming closer by the second.

He looked at her, and kept on looking, a hint of hunger in his eyes. He liked what he saw.

Or was it something else? Jess wondered. Did he think she was hot or was she becoming paranoid?

The man's eyes roved from her face to her hips and back again, and he openly ogled her as he went by.

Jess came close to whipping out her Beretta and bashing him across the face. Instead, she muttered, "Perv!" and walked on to her car. She glanced back and saw that he had stopped and was staring. "What?" she demanded. "Get lost, creepo."

The man smiled. "Are you always this stuck-up?"

Any other time, Jess would have been friendlier. He wasn't bad-looking. Far from it. But now she flipped him the finger and rasped, "I'm a cop, you idiot."

"And a pretty one at that." He winked and walked on.

Jess leaned on her car, feeling like the ultimate fool. She had to get a grip. She had to collect her wits and be as cool as ice when she told Delmarco about Larry. About to open her car door, she tensed. From somewhere close by came a clicking sound, like the clicking she had heard on her fire escape. Stepping back, she glanced right and left, then realized it was coming from under her car.

A bomb, Jess thought. She dropped to her hands and knees and almost screamed. For suddenly, she was nose to twitching nose with a large brown rat. They were known as Norway rats because it was once mistakenly believed they originated in Norway and spread around the world via shipping lanes. Only the last part was true. They really came from Asia.

This one was a foot and a half long, not including its eight-inch tail—as big and plump as a small dog. It was gnawing on a chicken bone, seeking to get to the marrow with its long teeth.

It was hard to say which of them was more surprised, but it was the rat that screeched and whirled and dashed off with incredible speed and agility.

"Jesus!" Jess breathed. Belatedly, she sensed she wasn't alone and heard the scrape of shoes. Jumping to the conclusion it must be the perv, she heaved upright, drew the Beretta as she rose, and extended it into the face of an extremely startled Dr. Frank.

"Whoa! It's me!"

"I can see that," Jess said curtly. "What the hell are you trying to do, get yourself shot?"

As he so often did, Dr. Frank answered her question with one of his own: "Do you always go around shooting people for no reason?"

Jess holstered her piece. "You shouldn't go around sneaking up on people, Doc. It could be hazardous." She eyed him closely. "What are you doing? Following me? Spying on me?"

"Walking to my car," Dr. Frank said and pointed at the one in the parking space next to hers. The customized license plate read SHRINK I.

"Oh."

"What were you doing on the ground. Are you okay?"

"I heard a noise. There was a rat underneath the car."

"Yes. Rats. We live near the water." Frank moved around her to his car and unlocked the door. "Remember my advice, Inspector Shepard. And be on time for your next session."

"How many times must I tell you I'm perfectly fine? What will it take for you to believe me?"

"I'm on your side, remember? So . . . see you next time," he said, defusing some of her anger with the simple phrase.

"Yes. Next time. See you." She couldn't help but laugh at the whole encounter. God only knew what a shrink would make of her holding a rat at gunpoint. Jess opened her car door and climbed in.

She inserted her key and flicked it to the right and the car turned over. Simultaneously, her radio blared to life at full volume, cranking out hard rock. Flinching, she stabbed at the volume control and turned the music down to a whisper.

Jess was rattled. She never listened to the station the radio was set to, and she never turned the volume that loud. When she had arrived for her appointment, she had been listening to the all-news station and had the radio so low, she could barely hear it. Now she looked all around.

"What the hell is going on?"

*   *   *

The sun was setting when Jess arrived at her apartment. Drained mentally and physically, she was eager to fill the tub and soak for an hour. But the moment she stepped inside her apartment, she went to the closet and took down her special box.

Sitting on the floor, Jess opened it and placed the dolls and other things to one side. It was the photos she wanted. Taking them out, she found the suicide photo of her father and studied it as she had countless times over the years. She saw his slumped body, saw the blood, saw smoke rising from a cigarette in an ashtray and, next to the ashtray, his cigarette lighter.

Jess peered into the box. In the corner was the lighter. She read the inscription aloud: " 'To a great cop. George Shepard. Number 870. Four twenty-two seventy-three. SFPD.' " The lighter had been given to him by John Mills as a token of their close friendship.

Mills. Jess suddenly had an overpowering urge to see him. He was the one person whose advice she could depend on. After replacing items in their box, she hurried back out, making a point of being sure her door was locked.

All the way to his place, Jess pondered how best to broach her dilemma. She rang the doorbell. When she entered, Jess found Mills at the top of the stairs in his bathrobe.

"Can we talk for a minute?" she asked.

"Jessica? This is unexpected. I was about to turn

in." Mills smiled his caring, paternal smile. "It must be important."

She nodded—rather animatedly, she feared.

"Come on up. You know I'd never turn you away."

Mills ushered Jess into his study. It radiated masculinity: old leather chairs, hardwood floors, wall paneling, plaques and trophies, and memories from his decades on the force. "Have a seat and I'll be back in a couple of minutes."

Jess sank into one of the chairs. Her fears were already fading. Mills would know what to do. He always did. She gazed out the window at the city skyline, barely aware of the passage of time, until a steaming cup of hot chocolate was held under her nose.

"With the marshmallow stuff you like on top." Mills sank into the other chair, holding a cup of his own.

"You're too wonderful for words."

Mills laughed that full, deep laugh of his. "I can count on one hand the number of people who ever said that to me." He took a sip. "So what brings you to my doorstep so late?"

"I wanted to talk about my father," Jess said. That wasn't at all what she really wanted to discuss, but she had to work up to it. She couldn't just blurt it out.

Mills frowned. "It's that shrink, isn't it? Don't let that shrink mess with your head."

"I was looking at the old photos," Jess said. "I just can't believe there was no warning, you know? That he just went off the deep end like that."

"Sometimes we don't see things right in front of our own noses," Mills said. "We're too close. Know what I mean?"

Jess thought of Larry and Bob, and nodded. "I wish he had told you he was going to kill all those men my mother had affairs with."

"Your father loved your mother very much. Loved her so much that it twisted him—do you understand?" Mills paused. "I have to admit, I always wonder . . . maybe if I hadn't told him about her . . . her affairs . . ."

That was news to Jess. "Wait!" She sat up with a start. "*You* told him? I didn't know that."

"He was my partner. You tell your partner everything. You tell him the truth. You back your partner. Always."

"Yes, but—" Jess was astounded that he never mentioned it before, although now that she thought about it, what difference did it make? It wasn't *how* her father learned about the affairs, it was what he *did* after he found out. She nodded to Mills that they understood each other. He did the same.

Then Mills said, "You need to focus on your case. Do your job. That's what matters."

"I'm on it."

"Okay." Mills drank more hot chocolate. "So.

Why else are you here? Is there something you need help with? A question you need answered?"

"You've already answered it," Jess told him.

"Really? Damn, I'm good."

Mills smiled, and Jess laughed, but deep down she was dreading tomorrow and what she had to do.

The day got off to a rotten start.

First, Jess couldn't find her car keys. She was positive they had been in her purse, but she found them under her windowsill. The window was locked, so she reasoned she had dropped them when she checked the fire escape right before she went to bed.

When she arrived at Homicide, Lieutenant Tabor immediately called her into his office. Wary of what he wanted, she took a seat, her body coiled like a steel spring. "Have I done something wrong?"

"No. Whatever made you ask that?" Tabor was in a good mood for once. "Since you were proven right on the serial link, you get to bring everyone else up to speed. Just in case the next vic they find fits your profile."

"Me? Why not Mike?"

"I should think you'd be flattered," the lieutenant said.

"Of course." But Jess didn't feel flattered. She felt frustrated and wary, and she dreaded what she had to do. She almost came right out with the truth

then and there. But she couldn't quite bring herself
to say it.

Lieutenant Tabor led her out, raised his arms,
and bellowed, "Listen up, people! Inspector Shepard
is going to fill you in on the latest serial
killing."

Mike Delmarco was at his desk. He smiled
encouragement.

Her stomach in a knot, Jess walked to her own
desk for her file and then back to the front of the
room, conscious of all eyes fixed on her. She was
nervous and she knew it showed, so she took a
deep breath, not sure where to start.

"Start with the signature," Mike whispered.

"Right." Jess started. "You all know about serial
killers taking trophies, a behavior that often gets
them caught. Well, there have been several cases in
the past where the killers got smart and didn't take
trophies. Instead, they 'signed' the bodies."

Jess removed several large photographs from
the file and pinned them to the wall. "It's been
done in different ways. With cuts. Brands. Burns.
Someone who marks a body like this will kill again
because killing's what he does. It's his art."

"So what do you suppose set this sicko off?"
Dale Becker broke in. "No-smoking signs?"

A few snickers resulted.

"Here are close-ups of our perp's signatures."
Jess pinned up photos of Bob's and Larry's burned
hands. "But signing a body like this isn't so smart,

after all. Because the signature itself can be your best clue." Looking over all the pictures she'd tacked up, Jess spotted one with the image of a woman's neck. There was a small red X on it. Just like the photos from those multiple homicides so many years ago. She became fixated on the picture and lost her train of thought about her current case.

"So cigarette burns," Mike said, jumping into the silence. "We gotta think we're looking for a smoker, and the overkill indicates rage, possibly personal in nature."

Jess turned back to her lecture and saw Dale Becker playing the class clown—as usual.

"Ooh, ooh, me, me!" Becker said.

She didn't want to dignify his behavior, and again Mike bailed her out. "Yeah?" he asked, raising his voice above the laughter caused by Becker.

"Yeah, um, has Inspector Shepard been eliminated as a suspect?" Dale replied.

Mike spun in his chair. "Funny, Dale."

"No, seriously. She slept with vic number one, right?" Dale responded. "Do we know if she slept with vic number two? I mean, he's kind of cute."

"That's enough!" Lieutenant Tabor commanded.

But it was too late. Jess was seething mad. She sprang toward Becker, her fists clenched. She didn't care if he was a foot taller and sixty pounds heavier. She was going to punch his lights out.

Dale rose to meet her, his own fists balled. "Come on! I dare you!"

Then Mike was there, wrapping his arms around Jess and pulling her away while others restrained Becker.

Lieutenant Tabor was furious. "I said enough! Delmarco, take your partner for some fresh air so she can cool off. Becker, in my office, right this second!"

Jess didn't resist. Her fury was fading fast. She couldn't stay mad when Dale Becker was only doing what they all should be doing and looking at the case from every angle.

Not until they were through the door and out in the corridor did Mike let go. "You're right. People who tell bad jokes should be strangled."

"Yeah, it was a bad joke." Jess read sympathy in his eyes—sympathy and perhaps a hint of something else. It achieved what all her hours of agonizing couldn't. Her inner wall was breached, and before she could stop herself, she heard herself saying, "And here's the punch line. I *did* sleep with victim number two."

Mike transformed to stone. He didn't blink, didn't seem to be breathing. After an eternity he softly asked, "Why would you do something like that?"

It wasn't the reaction Jess hoped for. "Look, it's not really any of your business who I sleep with."

"Who the hell cares who you sleep with?" Mike was angry, really angry, and he snarled, "I'm talking about you *lying* to me. Partners tell each other the truth."

"I didn't lie," Jess said lamely.

"Well, you definitely didn't tell me." Mike sat on a bench.

"I'm telling you now."

"It's not the same and you damn well know it. If two partners don't trust one another, then they shouldn't *be* partners."

"I trust you."

"Really?" Mike's mouth became a thin slash. "You sure have a hell of a strange way of showing it."

They glared at each other, an uncomfortable moment passing between them. Mike sighed and broke the silence.

"Right. So we have to tell the lieutenant."

"Can't we keep it between ourselves? Between partners? For now?" Jess was desperate to convince him.

"This connection could be important," Mike said. He saw her face, but he had to proceed with the case.

"Yeah, and it could be nothing."

"Jess, this is the first break we've had."

"That's not for us to decide."

The awful realization that this was the full truth and, after this truth, the full terrible truth would soon come out caused Jess to feel sick to her stomach. She sank. She tried to be strong. She tried not to give in to the panic roiling inside her. But she had pent up her feelings for so long, had contained them through sheer force of will, that now, with her inner barriers down, they poured from her like water spilling over a damn, and she did what she dearly desired not to: she groaned in anguish.

Mike gave her an earnest look. "Look, we don't have to tell the whole squad. Just the boss."

"And that's a good thing because . . . ?"

"His wife of twenty years just dumped him. I hardly think he's in a position to judge."

"It's not him I'm worried about."

"It will be all right. You'll see."

Jess raised her head. "Neither of us is that naive." She stood. "Give me a couple of minutes."

No one else was in the ladies' room. Jess composed herself and fluffed her hair, and when she looked halfway decent, she went back out and marched straight to the lieutenant's office. Mike fell into step beside her.

Tabor was searching in his desk for something, and grinned in greeting, still in his rare good mood. "If it isn't my rising star and her partner. What can I do for you on this fine morning?"

"Fine?" Mike said.

"The judge has awarded me visitation rights with my kids and halved my wife's alimony." Lieutenant Tabor was positively radiant. "It's the greatest day I've had in a good long while."

Jess cleared her throat. "I have something to tell you that might spoil it."

"Spit it out, Inspector Shepard. Nothing you say can possibly ruin this day for me."

Jess told him what she had to.

For a full minute, Tabor didn't speak, didn't move. Then he deflated like a punctured balloon. "Son of a bitch. I was wrong."

CHAPTER 9

The diner was a greasy spoon tucked away in the bowels of the waterfront. The waitresses were veterans of their trade, the food cheap. An eclectic mix of customers was present: longhaired students from the university, tattooed and pierced punks and Goths, a smattering of computer geeks, and a few businessmen.

"I come here for the pie," John Mills said. "The cook makes the best apple and cherry pies this side of Betty Crocker."

Jess was barely listening. Deep in the doldrums, she gazed out the window at passing pedestrians, wishing she were one of them. Wishing she had never had her one-night stands with Bob and Larry and the countless others.

Mike Delmarco and Lieutenant Tabor were also at the table, Mike nursing a cup of coffee and nibbling at a grilled cheese, Tabor with a plate of meat loaf in front of him he had hardly touched.

"With all due respect, sir," Tabor now said, "I didn't ask you here to talk about the food. We have a serious matter on the table."

"Lighten up, Lieutenant," Mills said. "There's never a problem that can't be solved, never a crisis that can't be smoothed over."

Tabor screwed his face into a grimace. "Yes, sir. But do you think this latest information is relevant?"

Mills forked a bite of apple pie into his mouth and chewed it before replying. "Too soon to say. But I doubt it. She said she, um, met both these guys in bars. It's likely the suspect is trolling the same places."

"I suppose." But Tabor didn't sound convinced. He turned to Jess. "Just to consider all options, any enemies? Anybody got a sick fixation on you, might be stalking you?"

Jess forced herself to stir, to answer. "I have been sort of feeling that I'm being watched. But I don't know anyone who would do something like this."

Lieutenant Tabor swiveled toward the commissioner. "I'm open to guidance here. I know how much her career means to you."

"How much *she* means to me," Mills amended. "And I appreciate the courtesy."

"So how do we handle this? Do we pull her from the case?"

Jess glanced at Mills, holding her breath, afraid he would say yes, yet at the same time afraid he would say no. Her career was in the balance. If Tabor pulled her, the captain would question why, and then everyone would learn about her sexual escapades.

Mills set his fork on his plate. "You operate as though this isn't a coincidence."

"But you just said—" Lieutenant Tabor began.

"That's the smart way to play it," Mills said, cutting him off. "So from that angle, pulling her off could tip the killer and blow a good lead. Also, if she *is* connected, you're gonna need her help to figure out how."

Tabor nodded, but expressed his concern. "It could put her at risk."

"She's a cop," Mills said. "She knows the risks."

"But this isn't routine," Mike argued. "This isn't what's required of her in the routine performance of her duties."

"We all go above and beyond, son," Mills said kindly.

"Sure. And we're all walking targets for every nutcase with a grudge. But this is different. You're not only endangering her—you're endangering everyone around her. Everyone she talks to."

Mills tilted his head at Mike. "Your concern is duly noted. But why don't we put it to Jessica? Why don't we ask if she's willing to go through with it?"

They all looked at her, and Jess nodded. "I want this case solved more than any of you. I'll do whatever it takes."

"Okay, then." Now that it had been decided, Lieutenant Tabor leaped right in. "We'll conduct a two-pronged investigation. One being the standard MCI Friends and Family, which I'll give to Becker and Sims." He stared at Jess. "The other is a little more personal. No one knows your personal life better than you do, so you and Mike are on that. Start looking into your extracurricular activities. Compile a list of everyone you've met. Look back at any and all odd occurrences, and maybe you'll see them in a new light. That sort of thing."

"Sounds like a plan to me," Mills said.

"And me," Jess agreed.

Delmarco drank some water.

"Well, I need to get back." Lieutenant Tabor extended his hand to Mills. "I want to thank you, Commissioner, for meeting like this on such short notice."

Silence fell after Tabor was gone. Mills finished his pie and they paid and walked out into a too-hot afternoon. The air was almost too still, as if the only thing that would move it was a violent upheaval from the Earth.

Jess touched Mike's arm. "Hang on a sec. . . ."

Nodding, Delmarco walked to their car.

Jess turned and walked toward Mills, who was

lingering at the curb. "Hey, thanks for backing me up in there."

Mills bestowed the sort of look he did when she had misbehaved as a child. "Backing you up? I was just giving my professional opinion. Want my *personal* opinion? What the hell are you doing?"

Flustered, Jess said, "I'm not doing anything."

"Yeah? That's not what I hear. These men you've been . . . 'seeing.' That scuffle with Culter. And earlier today you almost attacked an inspector."

"I didn't attack him. It was just a little disagreement."

"Not according to the version making the rounds." John Mills sighed. "Jessica, you're worrying me. I knew you were under stress. I figured it was the promotion and the Culter thing. I never, ever would have imagined."

Jess colored. "Don't go there."

"Why not? It's too personal? If it is so personal, why did I have to hear it through police channels and not directly from you?" Mills was snarling like an angry old bear. "Damn it, Jess. What are you trying to prove?"

Very seldom had Jess ever been mad at him, but she was mad now. "Don't judge me. I'm not trying to prove anything. I'm just trying to live my life."

"And it hasn't been an easy life." Mills softened. "Look, I'm only saying all this because you're so important to me. Because sometimes we have to be brutally frank with those who mean the most to us.

I'm worried, Jess. Honest to God worried. All these years I thought you had your head screwed on straight. Now you have me wondering."

A lump formed in Jess's throat. "I never wanted to hurt you."

Mills gave her a look that said she'd failed to accomplish that goal. At least, momentarily. "Uh-huh. And what's with you and this Delmarco genius?"

The comment made Jess recoil in surprise. She glanced over at Mike to make sure he hadn't overheard. Thankfully, he was busy with the radio and oblivious to the conversation.

"He's my partner," she stated flatly.

"Right. I know it's a new century now, and people seem to think it's okay to have sex with whoever. But don't shit where you eat. Got me? Keep your damn social life separate from your job."

"I do!" Jess was adamant.

Mills opened his mouth to say something, but apparently thought better of it.

"I'm telling you the truth," Jess vowed. "He's my partner, nothing more. He's never once stepped out of bounds."

"Let's hope he doesn't," Mills said. Was that a threat of some kind? He was a powerful man who could arrange situations that could make or break careers. Jess knew she was overreacting.

Jess covered his big hand with hers. "Look, John,

I know you worry about me, and I love you for it. But I can take care of myself."

"Really? Is that why people are dying all around you?"

"I will get things under control."

"See that you do, Jessica."

"Where do you want to begin?" Mike asked when she got in his car.

"The Saloon."

Jess sank back and idly viewed the scenery. She had a lot to think about. For starters, she was relieved the secret of her love life was safe for the moment, and grateful Tabor had seen fit to keep it under wraps.

Almost as if Delmarco were reading her thoughts, he commented, "I hope you won't mind my bringing this up, but maybe you're making a mountain out of a grain of sand."

"Come again?"

"You're obsessed with everyone finding out about your—what did the lieutenant call them?—extracurricular activities? But this isn't the Middle Ages. They don't label a woman a slut for sleeping with a man."

"Men. Plural," Jess corrected him. "And you're dead wrong. All the talk about women's equality and fairness in the workplace is a crock. Women are held to a different standard than men."

"*Playgirl*, anyone?" Mike said.

"Your point being that women are supposed to be as liberated as men? As free to indulge their fantasies? To explore their sexuality as they see fit?" Jess snorted in derision. "It doesn't work that way. Oh, sure, everyone gives it lip service, but in the real world, the world I live in, women who sleep around *are* branded sluts. Imagine what that would do to my career."

"I still think going to bed with two or three men is nothing to worry about."

"If only—" Jess said. "Let's just say that, yes, I'm obsessed about my personal life becoming public knowledge, and drop the subject, okay?"

"Whatever you want."

Mike was silent the rest of the way, which suited Jess fine. She was tired of talking about it. Yet she couldn't help but think about her mother. For years, she had thought how wrong it had been for her to sleep around, and now she was doing the exact same thing. Was it genetic? she mused. She preferred to think that in her case it was a combination of loneliness and physical need that drove her to haunt singles bars. Her mother, though, had no such excuse—not with her father right there in bed with her.

Jess had lost track of the number of times she had tried to make sense of it all: her mother cheating, her father going ballistic. A cruel cosmic joke had been played on their family, a joke that left her all alone in the world. She never had gotten over it.

Never could come to terms with the injustice of it all.

Deep in thought, Jess heard Delmarco ask, "You ready?" as they wheeled into the parking lot adjacent to the Saloon. The lot was empty save for two cars.

"Sure. Of course. Let's do it." Jess took the lead. Now that she had a decisive course of action, she felt invigorated. One way or another, she would find out who was responsible for turning her life topsy-turvy and make him pay.

Only one booth was occupied by early birds who appeared half hungover. The bartender wasn't anywhere to be seen, so Mike cupped a hand to his mouth. "Your attention, please. SFPD." When there was no response, he turned to Jess and said, "Did I say that out loud?"

A swinging door behind the counter opened and out came the bartender carrying a tray laden with clean glasses. He set it down and smiled, his gaze lingering on Jess. "What can I do for you?"

"Police. We need to ask you some questions," Mike said.

The bartender nodded at Jessica as he came around the end of the bar. "Hey, I know you. You're in here all the time. You're a cop? I don't believe it."

"Believe it," Jess said.

"What do you know?" The bartender chuckled. "I admit I thought you were pretty hot to be a working girl, but I couldn't figure why else you'd take off with those guys."

Jess thought she had her emotions under control, but she was wrong. Something inside snapped, and before she knew what she was doing, she grabbed him by the collar and slammed him against the wall. "Get it straight. We're not here to discuss your opinion of me. We're here to discuss a guy who used to look like this." From her jacket she took two photographs and showed one to him. It was of Larry before the murder. "And who now looks like this." She flashed a photo taken on the beach.

The bartender gulped. "Jesus."

"Now I know for a fact that this guy spent time here," Jess said. "So what I wanna know is, did you ever see him with anybody?"

"Hey." The bartender held up both hands. "Don't see no evil, hear no evil."

"When I want a monkey, I'll ask for one."

The bartender glanced at Mike for help. He got none. "What is this? Some sort of cop scam you're trying to run?"

"What?" Jess tightened her grip on his collar.

"Look, the only person I ever saw him leave the bar with, aside from his girlfriend, was you."

Mike edged in. "No one else? Ever?"

"Why would I lie? But keep in mind this place is a madhouse most nights. Around closing time, I'm so busy, it keeps me hopping just getting the tabs

Edmund Culter gets the upper hand on Jessica Shepard…
for the moment.

Jess is forced to work through her issues with
Dr. Melvin Frank.

Jessica and her mentor, Police Commissioner John Mills.

Mike Delmarco, Jessica's new partner in Homicide Division.

Jess rummages through photographs of her dark family past.

Mike and Jessica work a Pac Bell Park crime scene.

Lieutenant Tabor.

Jess takes exception to Dale Becker's accusations that she might be the killer they are after.

The strain of
the job and the
deaths sur-
rounding her
begin to wear
on Jess.

Mike, Mills, and Jess try to work through their theories
on the case.

Mike and Jess becoming more than just partners.

Mike is forced to ask Jess some hard questions about her
relationships with the victims.

Accused of the murders, Jess sits in prison, awaiting her hearing.

Mike swoons after being drugged.

Jess finally faces down the real killer.

paid up. For all I know, he could have gone home with a different babe every night."

"You can't remember any others? You're sure?"

"Maybe he left with Shirley once. She works as a computer programmer somewhere. That's the best I can do."

Jess knew a dead end when she encountered one. "We're wasting our time." She dropped the bartender hard, and walked out. Mike followed, making no apologies for his partner.

"Geber's apartment next?" he asked.

"Why not?" Jess rejoined. "But I go in alone."

"We're partners, as you conveniently keep forgetting."

"Think about it a minute."

He did, and didn't object when she left him by the car and knocked on the apartment office to have the landlady open the room. It was exactly as she remembered, only messier. Larry had a thing about not washing dishes; he had left a mountain of dirty plates and bowls piled in the sink. He also had a thing about not doing laundry. Enough dirty clothes littered the floor to keep the Salvation Army in business for a year.

"He always was a slob," the landlady remarked.

Jess conducted a cursory sweep, then examined several framed photographs, all of the same woman. The girlfriend, she suspected, since in two of the photos Larry and the woman were sucking face.

"Bastard never paid his rent on time," the landlady sniffed. "Played drums all night."

"Is that so?" Jess moved to the window and saw Mike. He wasn't alone. He was talking to Wilson Jefferson, her old patrol partner.

"Serves him right. You know what I mean?" the landlady said.

Jess turned. "Did Larry have many regular visitors?"

"He had a steady, but he wasn't very faithful." She jangled her keys. "Oh, I'd peek out now and then when I'd hear him drive up, just to see, you know." She paused. "The last person I saw him with looked a lot like you."

Jess returned the landlady's stony stare and quickly turned away. She wasn't always as tough as she wanted to be.

"Seemed like he would screw any skank who came on to him," the landlady said.

"If anyone shows up asking about him, try to get their names and addresses. It's important."

"I'll see what I can do, but don't expect miracles."

CHAPTER 10

Jessica's old partner was gone when she reached the street. "So you and Wilson—you guys are getting pretty tight, huh?"

Mike grinned. "Never be as tight as you and Wilson."

Jess's skin prickled as if from a heat rash. "I didn't sleep with him," she said defensively.

"Didn't say you did."

"But you were thinking it, right?"

Mike acted stunned. "What's going on? You're putting words in my mouth for no reason."

"Am I?" Jess was being unfair, but she couldn't help herself. She had read something in his eyes, a wariness that hadn't been there before.

"Find anything up there?" Mike tried to divert her.

Jess let him. "Looks like we just wasted all day tracking down me."

"At least we have a suspect now."

If looks could kill, she'd have been responsible for at least one homicide.

"Aw, come on, Jess. I'm just joking."

"Screw you, Mike." Jess climbed in the passenger side and slammed the door. A throbbing in her temples heralded a headache, the kind that sometimes turned her into a vegetable. She refused to look at him when he slid behind the wheel.

"Where to now?"

"Take me home."

"How about I treat you to a bite to eat? Or a drink?"

"You don't want to be seen in public with me," Jess said. "Think of all the gossip behind your back."

"Damn it, I don't deserve this raking over the coals. I'm your partner. I'm the one person you can count on."

"I want to believe that," Jess bluntly informed him.

"What about Wilson?"

"What about him?"

"Can you count on him?" Mike asked.

"Wilson proved himself by always covering my back when I needed it covered. So, yeah, I can. You? I think you're there for me. You've covered for me with the lieutenant—more than once."

Ticked off, Mike gunned the motor. "But?"

"But the chips haven't been totally down yet. So I don't know."

"Well, you better know soon, Shepard. 'Cause we're gonna solve this thing and I gotta know you'll be covering my back."

"Don't worry, Delmarco," she answered. "I won't let you die."

The rest of the ride home was quiet. Mike didn't even say good night when he dropped her off. She was mad at herself for being mad at him, and so preoccupied with guilt, she mechanically slid her key into her lock and twisted. But nothing happened. There was no telltale click.

Jess realized the door was already unlocked. She entered quietly and dropped her keys on the table. Palming the Beretta, she headed toward the living room, where she thought she heard furtive rustling. She moved in a combat crouch, sweeping her weapon from wall to wall.

A soft tinkle came from the kitchen—the clink of ice in a glass. Weapon at the ready, Jess crept toward it, not knowing whom to expect, but certainly not the man she saw pouring himself a drink. "What the hell are you doing here?"

Jimmy Schmidt stopped pouring and raised a hand in mock terror. "Eek! Don't shoot!"

"How did you get in here?" Jess had the Beretta centered on his chest.

"Is that any kind of welcome for a man who's seen you naked?" Smirking and obviously drunk,

Jimmy showed her a lock pick. "Handy little tools, these."

"Why are you in my house, Jimmy?"

Something in her tone made Jimmy place the glass on the table and hold his hands up, palms out. "You tell me. You're the hotshot inspector."

Jess lowered her gun, but didn't take her eyes off Jimmy.

"Aw, come on, I'm just kidding. I wanted to see you, that's all. It's just . . . I miss you." Then, like a puppy whining for attention and approval, he asked, "Don't you miss me, Jess?"

Jess put the Beretta on the table and leaned on it, her fatigue catching up with her. "Jimmy, I told you. It's over. Okay?"

Adopting his usual cocky air, Jimmy strutted around the table and brazenly molded his hands to her backside. "Are you sure?"

"I've never been more sure of anything in my life. Now move those mitts or lose your fingers."

Jimmy sniffed her hair. "Damn, you smell good."

"What do you think you're doing?" Jess barked.

He answered her question by pulling her toward him. Jess responded with a few moves of her own.

Grabbing his wrist and his upper arm, she pivoted and flipped him clean over her shoulder, slamming him hard to the floor. Jimmy squawked and immediately attempted to get back up. Streaking her *yawara* from its sheath, she struck him across the bridge of his nose. Down he went, onto his back, his nose bleeding profusely.

"What the fuck?"

Snatching up her Beretta, Jess pinned him with one knee and jammed the pistol against his head. "Is it you?" she hissed.

"Me what?"

"*Is it you?*" Jess was close to the edge. She would gladly shoot him if he gave her the slightest excuse.

"Me what? Jesus Christ. Calm down!"

Jess whacked him with the Beretta, not hard enough to knock him out, but hard enough to demonstrate she was serious. "Is it? Are you screwing with me, Jimmy? Because it isn't just my job you're messing over—it's my life! And I will kill you before I let that happen."

"What in God's name are you talking about?" Jimmy had a hand clamped to his nose in an effort to stem the bleeding.

"You don't know?" Jess barked, then saw clearly that he didn't. She also clearly saw her reflection in the window. Holding him down, hitting him—she looked like a crazed perp. Straightening, she backed off. "You really don't," she whispered, more to herself than Jimmy.

"All I know is that you're a psychopath." Jimmy rose, his mouth and chin crimson. "You got a screw loose."

Jess took a step toward him. "I'm sorry."

"Don't touch me!" Jimmy backed off, groped on

the sink for a dishcloth, and pressed it to his nose. "You've done enough damage for one night." The cloth muffled his words.

"You don't understand."

Spinning, Jimmy stormed off. "This is what I get for thinking you still feel for me like I feel for you. Bitch."

"Dick," Jessica answered, matching his indignation.

Jimmy tossed the bloody towel on the floor and moved toward the door. The walls shook when he slammed it shut.

Jess's bravado sagged with her body as she slumped into a chair and dipped her chin on her chest. "What have I done?" she asked the floor. Smears of bright blood glistened wetly. Taking a clean dish towel, she began wiping the blood up. But her mind wasn't on what she was doing. It was on what Dr. Frank would say if she told him. What was it he claimed she had? Anger issues to deal with? Maybe she should listen to him for once. But almost in the next thought, she decided Frank was still mistaken. She couldn't be blamed for defending herself. Jimmy had been irresponsible: breaking and entering, harassing her, groping her. He was the one who had done wrong and he should count himself lucky to have gotten off as lightly as he had.

Once the floor was clean, Jess dropped the towel in a trash can in the corner and poured herself a drink. She cracked the window and sat staring out blankly at the night.

As bad as things were, Jess mused, they could be a lot worse. So far no one had unearthed her dirty little secret. The secret that could ruin her career. And if she had no career, she had no life. Which reminded her. She phoned Mike and, when his answering machine answered, simply said, "This is Shepard. I have an appointment in the morning. I'll be about an hour late."

Jess hung up. The gamble she was contemplating was a big one, but she had to find out in advance of the trial. She had to know if her career was in jeopardy.

Edmund Culter's sneer was as vicious as ever. "Well, well, well. The girl scout comes calling. Bring any cookies?" He came to the cell bars. "I was wondering how long it would take."

"You've been expecting me?" Jess chalked it up to more mind games on his part. "Not likely."

"Play me for a chump, if you want, but I know the truth about you." Culter was smug and cocky. "I've seen into the dark depths of your soul and discovered my psychic twin."

"You're so full of shit, it's not funny."

"Am I? Then let's hear why you came." Culter leaned against the bars. "Make it really good."

"How much have you told them?"

Culter cackled with glee. "I knew it! You're worried. You should be. I've told them enough. My attorney, anyway."

"Does your lawyer know what really happened that night?"

Instead of answering, Culter gripped the bars and pressed his face between two of them. "When did you first realize you had the capacity to kill?"

"What?"

Culter caressed one of the bars, stroking it up and down. "We all have it in us. It's just a matter of who can control it. Can you?"

His arrogance threw her. "I won't be played for a chump, either."

"Think so?" Culter laughed, a cold, hard, vicious laugh. "Remember, your secret is my secret. You shouldn't lie like that."

"I can see this will get me nowhere."

"You thought I'd make it easy? After what you did?" Culter touched his face where she had kicked it. "I can't wait for the truth to come out. I hope they crucify you, bitch. I hope they fry you and throw you out on your ass."

"Nice talking to you again, too," Jess said, and turned to get out of there. She was violating procedure and it wouldn't do for her to be caught. But she only took a step when the worst that could happen did.

"Jessica! Hold it right there!"

Ray Porter barreled toward her like an angry bull. His suit, his tie, and his shoes were as immaculate as always. "What the hell are you doing here with my client?"

"Homicide work, Ray," Jess said. "Just following up on some hunches."

"Then you go through me. You ask my permission. I want to be here when you talk to him. At all times. You got that?"

Culter was enjoying their exchange. "Better listen to him, twin. Remember, the only way to silence him in court is to kill him."

"Edmund!" Porter admonished his client. Then he said to Jess, "Remember what I told you! Only in my presence."

Jess tried to diffuse things. "No need to throw a hissy fit. Whatever you want is cool by me."

Ray's hostility melted and was replaced by his oily smile. "Just protecting my client. You're in for a real battle on this one."

Jess tried to act nonchalant. "Really?"

"Jess, I'm gonna have to come at you with both guns blazing."

"Me?" Jess feigned innocence. "What did I do?"

Ray leaned closer. "The law works in mysterious ways, Jess. It's not always as simple as rounding up the bad guys."

"What the hell does that mean?"

"I'll explain it to you. In detail." Ray leaned closer yet. "But this is not the right time or place."

Jess came close to slugging him. Not because of the hungry gleam in his eyes or how he was practically brushing against her, but for his underhanded tactics.

"And I suppose you have a suggestion as to what is? The time and place, I mean."

Ray made certain no one was near. "Come over to my house Sunday morning, and we can talk about it. You know, like old times." He sniffed like a dog in heat. "I like your perfume."

"Talk, Ray. That's all."

"You never know." Porter smoothed his jacket and walked off with a bounce in his step.

"Pig," Jess said under her breath. She took a deep breath and regained a modicum of composure. Turning, she took a step, then stopped as if she had slammed into a brick wall. "Mike!"

Delmarco was on the stairs. Hands in his pockets, he slowly descended. His face was hard to decipher.

"What are you doing here? Spying on me?"

"I was using the stairwell to get from Homicide to the lobby and heard Porter yell your name. Thought I'd come on down and see what was up."

Jess stared after the lawyer. "He gives scum a whole new meaning. Sometimes I could kill that guy."

Mike's reserve was glaringly obvious. "Well, I guess we should get started."

"I guess so."

She was sorry for offending him the day before, yet angry he was obviously making her pay for her behavior. They'd have to find a way to work through this sometime during the day, or they would accomplish little else than sniping at each other. She knew she'd have to apologize sooner or later, so she steeled herself for the day ahead.

Things worked out between them in the end, although Jess and Mike made little headway on the case. Mike dropped her off at the station. She wanted to run some other angles in her mind.

Climbing the stairs to Homicide, Jess stopped first into the small office reserved for the coffeemaker, a small fridge, and a table. Her mug was on the peg she had been assigned, and she took it down to fill it. As she did, she heard a sound from inside the cup. Puzzled, she looked down, and flushed red-hot with fury.

At the bottom of the cup was a condom.

"Something the matter, Inspector Shepard?" Dale Becker was in the doorway, sipping coffee of his own.

Jess jumped at his voice. "Jesus, you scared the shit out of me. Everything is just fine. Thank you." She threw the condom into the trash, rinsed out her cup, and filled it with coffee. "Excuse me. You're blocking the way." Dale stepped aside, but at a snail's pace, taunting her.

Half a dozen detectives were busy at work. Jess nodded at Parker and sat down. Without her noticing, Dale had been nipping at her heels, and now was beside her desk. "Do you want something?" she asked.

"Yup. Working late. Still going over all those unanswered questions," Dale said. "Such as, why didn't you come out and say early on that you knew the second victim? Such as, what else haven't you told us? And the biggest question of all. The one that has me stumped the most. Why is someone who would normally be considered a prime suspect allowed to participate in the investigation?"

"You'll have to take that up with the lieutenant."

"No, I'm taking it up with you, here and now, Shepard." Dale's tone was an insult in itself.

Jessica put down her coffee. "If you wanna say something to me, Dale, stop being a pussy and just come right out and say it."

Dale bent down. "I know about you. I know about you and Bob. And I also know about you and Larry. Let me ask you: while you were sleeping with them, were you thinking about hitting them?"

Jess started to come up out of her chair. She had put up with all she was going to tolerate from him. But a sudden change in his expression stopped her. He *wanted* her mad. He *wanted* her to do something, to take a swing or otherwise prove she was as prone to violence as he implied.

"Are you thinking about hitting me now?" Dale goaded. "Go ahead. You know you want to."

Jess sat back down.

Dale couldn't hide his disappointment. "I don't

know what's going on with this case. But I do know one thing for sure. Every bone in your body wants to hit me just now. Am I right?"

Jess just sat there, willing herself to keep still. She didn't want to play his game any longer. Knowing he'd won, Becker walked off smiling.

Jess suddenly gasped for breath. She hadn't realized she'd stopped breathing during Becker's taunting. Gulping in the stagnant air of the Homicide Division, she returned to an uneasy calm. God knew how long it would be until she would really be calm again. The worst part was that Becker was right. The one thing she had wanted to do more than anything was take a swing at him. To say this bothered her was an understatement.

She took a deep breath and tried to analyze what had just happened.

It was no use denying the truth about her night with Larry. But for the life of her, she was stumped as to how Dale found out. Lieutenant Tabor had promised to keep it quiet, and Mills certainly wouldn't broadcast it. That left one person, and one person alone: Mike Delmarco.

Seagulls were perched on pilings near Delmarco's house when Jessica pulled up. One flew over and landed near her. From the way it stared, she assumed it wanted food. "Sorry. I don't have any."

Jess walked to the door, in the grip of inner turmoil. For all his repeated talk about how important it was for partners to back partners, Mike had gone and betrayed her. She knocked and called out, "Mike?"

"Who is it?"

"It's me, Jess."

"Hey, come in, the door's open. Hey, stranger, welcome."

The interior was nicely furnished. Mike was at a counter that separated the kitchen and the living room, doing paperwork. He came to meet her, saying, "Have a seat. I'll be a couple of minutes yet."

"We need to talk." Jess pushed against his chest, moving him back to the counter. "There are a few things we need to get clear, *partner*."

"What's eating you?" His confusion seemed genuine.

"How could you?" Jess's anger was seeping through. "How could you do that?"

"What are you talking about?"

"Don't play innocent!" Jess had grown to like him, to like him a lot, which made his betrayal all the more bitter. She refused to cry even though she wanted to. She refused to let him see that she cared.

"I honestly have no idea what you're talking about." Mike reached for her, but she swatted his hand.

"Dale. You told him about me and the victims. Mike, I was starting to trust you!"

Mike blinked. "I can't believe it. You think I'd do something like that. What's the matter with you?"

"You've been treating me coldly since yesterday," Jess said. "Now this. What else am I to think?"

"Can you blame me after you reamed me for no reason?" Mike countered.

Jess stared deep into his eyes. Her intuition kicked in, and she saw that she had unjustly accused him. "Sorry," she said softly. All she seemed to do lately was apologize. She turned to go.

Suddenly, Mike was in front of her. "Where are you going? Get in here. We've got work to do."

Jess turned and joined Mike in the living room. Now there was one more mystery to solve in this case.

"Since you didn't tell him and I sure as hell didn't tell him, who did? Only two other people know, the lieutenant and John Mills."

"John would never do anything to hurt me."

"I agree. So that leaves Lieutenant Tabor, who isn't exactly the most tight-lipped person we know, is he?"

Now that Jess thought about it, it would be just like Tabor to let it slip. "God, I am such an idiot."

Mike gripped her shoulders and steered her to a stool. "We all have our bad days. You're just having a bad month. Have a seat while I wrap things up. Want some java?"

"Sure," Jess said. He already had a pot made,

and poured her a cup. Near them on a wall hung several long fishing poles. On the floor under the poles sat a tackle box. "You fish? Somehow I can't picture it."

"I used to nearly every day. It's about the most relaxing thing I know other than—" Mike stopped himself and set the cup in front of her along with a spoon and a bowl of sugar. "But I don't have much time to relax these days."

"You continue to be a bundle of surprises, Inspector Delmarco."

"I hope they're nice surprises, Inspector Shepard."

Was it Jess's imagination, or was he coming on to her?

CHAPTER 11

The next day was all uphill for Jess.

They visited Bob Sherman's condo. Sherman had been a photographer and photographs were everywhere: piled on the floor, tacked to the walls, in file cabinets, stacked on end tables.

"Did he take any of you?" Mike casually inquired while thumbing through a handful.

"I'm not *that* kinky," Jess said.

"Most of these are nature scenes. Looks like he canvassed the entire city for spots to shoot. Must be how he found that stand of trees he took you to."

"Must be." Jess hadn't thought of that.

They searched for an address book, a list of names, anything that would give them a line on Sherman's friends and acquaintances.

"Not a damn thing," Mike said as he closed the last dresser drawer. "He must have kept it all in his head."

Jess had found a trunk. It was filed with photos, most in color, but some in black and white. She flicked through them: nature scene after nature scene, many involving wildlife. There were seals, sea lions, pelicans. She plunged her hand in deeper and came out with a new handful. One was of the Golden Gate Bridge. Another was a wharf. The third was a strip of shore. She was about to drop it into the trunk when the background caught her eye. "This is interesting."

Mike came around the bed. "What is?"

"Is it me, or is this the area where we found Bob's body?"

It only took one glance for Mike to nod and say, "It sure as hell is. Another of life's little ironies."

"So you think it's coincidence?"

Mike waved an arm to encompass the photographs in the trunk and on the wall and a mountain of photos on the bedroom floor. "As many as this guy took? I wouldn't be surprised if we find one of the spot where Larry Geber's body was discovered."

"It would take forever to go through all of these," Jess said.

"We'll let Dale and Sims have the honor. It will get Dale out of the station so he can't hassle you as much."

"How thoughtful you are, kind sir."

Their next stop was Homicide. While Mike called down to the medical examiner's office to see if the test results were in, Jessica ran a computer search to see if similar murders had been reported from anywhere else in the country. It was the proverbial long shot. But the FBI had firmly established that most serial killers never stayed in one place for long, for obvious reasons. Her search, however, netted no matches.

It was then that Lieutenant Tabor called them into his office for an update. "I was hoping for more results," he said after hearing of the dead ends they had run into.

Jess had her opening. "And I was hoping no one would hear about me and Larry Geber, but it seems none of our wishes are coming true, sir."

Tabor had been about to pop an antacid pill into his mouth. "Excuse me? What are you implying, Inspector Shepard?"

"I'm not implying anything," Jess said. "But Becker confronted me about it last night. Mike didn't say anything to him, and I sure as hell didn't, so that narrows the list of suspects—so to speak."

"And you think it was me?"

"You're the likeliest source."

Lieutenant Tabor put the pill in his mouth, washed it down with water, then smacked the glass onto his desk, spilling some. "I don't believe what I'm hearing. I was the one who suggested the private meeting with the commissioner, if you'll recall. I was the one who wanted to keep everything under wraps."

Mike rallied to her defense. "Are you sure you didn't maybe let it slip by mistake? Or that Becker might have overheard you discussing it with someone?"

"Commissioner Mills did phone me late yesterday," Lieutenant Tabor said, "and my door might have been open. Maybe Becker eavesdropped."

Jess was more interested in the other tidbit of information. "What did John Mills want?"

"To see how you were doing. And to reassure me I did the right thing by keeping you on the case." Tabor drummed his fingers on his desk. "It must be nice to have a fairy godfather to watch over you."

"It has its perks." Jess was flattered that Mills was so concerned, but she was also slightly resentful that he apparently thought she needed close watching. Evidently, he didn't think she could manage on her own.

"I'm waiting," Lieutenant Tabor said.

"For what?" Jess said, and then it hit her. "Oh. I'm sorry I wrongly accused you. If it's any consolation, I'm batting zero for two times at bat."

"Translation, please."

Mike answered for her. "She accused me, too."

"Ah." Tabor fluttered his lips. "Get your act together, Shepard. Wild assumptions only fuel Dale

Becker's contention that you don't belong here. And he's a bulldog when he has a beef."

"I'll keep that in mind," Jess promised.

When the end of their shift rolled around, Mike invited her to dinner. Tired and hungry, she accepted.

"Great. I know just the place. Follow me," Mike said when they got to their cars.

She was surprised when he led her back to his place. They entered and Mike poured her a drink, then got to work in the kitchen.

Jess settled into a comfortable chair, enjoying the momentary peace. Unbidden, John Mills's stern warning rang in her mind: *Keep your damn social life separate from your job.* So did Lieutenant Tabor's tactlessly frank *Don't sleep with him.* But all she was doing was spending some downtime with her partner, nothing more.

While Mike prepared salmon, mashed potatoes, and a salad, Jess moved to the end of the counter and related how hard her childhood had been. "Growing up without parents is a bitch. Oh, sure, John was always there for me, but I couldn't go to him with certain stuff. With the kind of problems girls only talk about with their mothers."

"He must have done something right," Mike said while tossing the said. "You turned out okay."

"Just okay, huh?" Jess grinned. "Yes, he stood by me when no one else would. My father's brother, my mom's sisters, they wanted nothing to do with me. They treated me like I had something to do with my father's breakdown. Like I was somehow partly to blame."

"That's bogus. You were just a kid."

"I remember my father's brother taking me aside at the funeral and asking me if my father had ever said anything to me about my mother?"

"About her affairs, you mean?" Mike said while sprinkling seasoning on the sizzling salmon.

"Yes, about—" Jess straightened. "Wait a minute. How did you know? I never told you."

"I always do a background check on my partners, remember? So I know what I'm letting myself in for."

"You went through my personnel file?" Jess was appalled. It was a personal as well as a departmental no-no.

"There are other ways." But Mike didn't elaborate. What he did do was take a spatula and slide large pieces of salmon onto two plates and then add the mashed potatoes and salad. "Here you go. I caught and smoked this salmon myself with my bare hands in shark-infested waters."

"Yeah, right." Jess forked a bite into her mouth and slowly chewed. "Mmmm. Delicious. You could spoil a girl, easy."

"The right girl, I wouldn't mind."

Jess tried the mashed potatoes and the salad. "If you ever give up being a cop, become a cook. You've got real talent."

"Anything but an ambulance chaser would be fine by me," Mike remarked.

It made Jess think of Ray Porter, and filled her with keen regret that she ever slept with him. Or Jimmy Schmidt.

"Why the frown? I thought I have talent?"

"I'm starting to realize I have more enemies than I thought," Jess said.

Mike chuckled. "Everybody has more enemies than they think."

In that regard, Jess considered herself an expert. "My whole life, all I've ever wanted was to work on a homicide case. And now I can't wait until it's over."

"Don't let it get to you. Listen, sometimes a case practically clears itself. Other times, for no reason at all, it's like pulling teeth. And it's got nothing to do with you."

"This one does."

"Only because of circumstances over which you have no control. You're a good inspector. The only reason that guys like Dale give you grief is that they're afraid you might be better than them." Mike stabbed a piece of salmon, but instead of putting it in his mouth, he held the fork out to her.

The intimate gesture was not lost on Jess. She slid the salmon into her mouth with the tip of her tongue, and smiled. "What about you?"

"There's no chance you're better than me."

They laughed, and Jess gazed at him with new-found fondness. "Oh, yeah? And why is that?"

"Because you bring out the best in me, partner."

The compliment was so sweet, and so unexpected, Jess drank some wine to cover her embarrassment. He held his glass out and she clinked it with her own. "Partner," she toasted.

"I love the way you eat."

Jess was thrown for a loop. "Where did that come from?"

"The way you shovel it in," Mike said. "I've never seen a woman go at it like that before."

She paused. "John would never really tell me much about my mother. It didn't matter what I asked him—it was a complete no-fly zone. Except at dinner he said I eat just like her. Two-fisted. What can I say? I like to eat."

"Me, too."

Jess liked it when Mike reached across the counter and stroked her hair. But then he leaned forward and kissed her on the mouth. Paralyzed with indecision, she didn't know what to do. She didn't mind him kissing her. Quite the opposite. But the admonitions of her superiors were fresh in her memory. Pulling back, she stood up and absently moved toward a desk, her emotions in a tug of war.

"I'm sorry," Mike said. "I shouldn't have."

"No, it's all right," Jess replied, keeping her back to him so he wouldn't see how shaken she was.

"You should have popped me one," Mike said.

"I still can," Jess playfully warned. Her gaze strayed to the wall above the desk. To several Post-its, one of which had DR. MELVIN FRANK written on it in bold block letters, along with Frank's phone number. Dumbfounded, she took it down and stared at it.

"Come on back and finish your meal. I promise to behave myself."

Whirling, Jess marched over and slapped the note down next to his plate. "Dr. Frank?"

Mike withered like a plant under a burning sun. "Oh, God."

"Why are you talking to my shrink, Mike? Comparing notes?"

"It's not what you think."

Jess shoved him, hard. "Oh, it's exactly what I think. So this is how you knew about my mother? Comparing notes with the good doctor on the side?"

"No." Mike tried to grasp her hand but she jerked back. "You're taking this all wrong. Trust me."

"What a laugh!" Jess declared, but she didn't feel like laughing. "Everyone keeps saying the same thing. Dr. Frank, you, the lieutenant. But none of you can be trusted."

"Why don't we talk this out?"

"So you can feed me more lies? My gullibility only extends so far." Wheeling, Jess made for the front door. "Don't bother walking me out. In fact, don't call me or come anywhere near me except in the line of duty." She glanced over her shoulder. "Is that clear, *partner*?"

"Perfectly."

Jess reached her apartment in record time. She was so incensed, she broke the speed limit every mile of the way, doing seventy-five and eighty on the straight stretches. She felt like she was moving that fast on foot, too, as she barreled down the hallway to her apartment.

Much to her amazement, a huge bouquet of red roses was propped against her door. "Now what?" Jess said, and plucked a note attached to the stems. " 'Sorry about whatever,' " she read. " 'Thinking of you. Relaxation? Come see me tomorrow. I'm here for you. Ray Porter.' " The card had Ray's initials embossed in bold gold letters.

"Assholes! Assholes! Assholes!" Jess fumed. She didn't give a flying fig if anyone heard her. Unlocking her door, she tossed the roses into the sink. It was stuffy, so she unlatched her window and raised it to let in some air. The instant she did, she heard a clicking sound from below.

Jess poked her head out to inspect the fire escape. The alley was an inky soup. She saw nothing to account for the clicking and was easing her head back inside when something or someone moved at the bottom of the fire escape.

"Who's there?"

The clicking ceased.

"Did you hear me? I'm a cop."

Among the shadows a darker shadow detached itself and flowed toward the mouth of the alley. Footsteps pattered on the pavement.

"Hold it!" Jess was out the window in a flash, bounding down the metal steps. She held on to the rail with one hand and drew her Beretta with the other. She still had a few steps to go when she launched herself into the air and hit the ground running.

A figure was silhouetted in the mouth of the alley. All Jess had was the briefest of glimpses, a suggestion of a man, hunched over. "Police! Stop where you are!" But the prowler kept on running.

At the street, Jess turned right, as her quarry had done. The sidewalks weren't crowded. A fleeing figure should stand out, but she didn't see him. Several people she passed saw the Beretta and drew back. "Police!" she yelled to put them at ease. "Did a man go running by?"

An elderly man pointed at the next intersection. "He went around there."

Jess poured on the speed. She reached the inter-section well before the prowler could possibly reach the far end of the block, but he was nowhere to be seen. Thinking he had ducked into a door-way, she stalked from building to building but came up empty-handed. Whoever it was had given her the slip.

Turning, Jess retraced her steps. The chase wasn't a total waste. She had a witness. But when she came to where the elderly man had been, he was gone. She wanted to kick herself for not telling him to stay put.

Jess went down the alley. She scoured the spot where the lurker had been, but there were no cigarette or cigar butts, no discarded gum wrappers or food containers, nothing that would give her a lead on the man's identity.

Tiredly climbing the fire escape to her window, Jess slipped inside, closed it, and worked the latch.

The roses in the sink reminded her of unfinished business. She opened a cupboard. The vase she was looking for wasn't there. She opened the next, said, "Ah!" and filled it with enough water to keep the roses fresh for a few days.

From a drawer inside the sink, Jess took out a pair of scissors and began trimming the stems. "The bozo who bought you might be a butthead, but that doesn't mean I let you die. Nothing should die before its time."

Jess opened the fridge, grabbed a bottle of orange juice, and took a couple of swigs. She started to tap Ray Porter's phone number on her cell phone, but second thoughts stopped her. She decided to get back to the task at hand and give the roses a fitting home. She had half of them done and was reaching for another when she felt a sharp sting of a thorn in her finger. A bubble of blood mushroomed; she washed it off under the tap.

"The perfect cap to a rotten day," Jess said. "And listen to me? I'm talking to myself like a regular loon."

She snipped the thorn. Suddenly, from outside her window, came a metallic clicking. The stalker was back! His arrogance was unbelievable. But this time he wasn't getting away.

Jess started to turn, and gasped. Once again the world was blurring; a black void was devouring the kitchen. She took half a step, the strength draining from her body like water from a sieve. *No!* she inwardly screamed. She wouldn't let it happen again.

Gritting her teeth, Jess resisted passing out. Her legs wobbled, and she gripped the sink to keep from falling. "Not this time!" she declared.

Suddenly, Jess was aware that the clicking had grown louder. The stalker was coming up the fire escape. Mewing like a kitten, so weak she could barely move her arm, she tried to draw the Beretta.

That was the last thing she remembered.

CHAPTER 12

Fog was everywhere. Misty tendrils writhed about Jessica like snakes. She didn't know where she was, but she sensed she was in great danger. Footsteps scraped nearby, and she impulsively inquired, "Is anyone there?"

Heavy breathing fell on her ears. Jess peered into the thick gray veil, but it was like peering into a dense cloud of smoke.

More footsteps scuffed the ground, closer now, and from the sound, whatever was out there was circling her.

Jess bolted, fleeing as fast as her legs would carry her, scared to death that at any instant she would slam into a building or a car or some other obstacle. When the footsteps and the heavy breathing had faded far behind her, she stopped to catch her breath.

Almost immediately came the sound of more

footsteps, of more heavy breathing. Dread crept over Jess as she frantically sought to pinpoint the source. A shape materialized—a monstrous shape lumbering slowly toward her. She backed away, walking at first, then running. But the thing was running, too, matching her step for step.

Without warning Jess slammed into a brick wall or something like it. Her feet swept out from under her and down she went. Fear filled her, and she sought to push to her feet. But now the thing was right next to her and large hands or paws were stretching toward her throat.

Just then a car horn blared.

Jessica's eyes snapped open. She was on her back, her arms and legs spread-eagle, staring at the kitchen ceiling. Her throat was parched dry and her ears were ringing. She sat up, her back against a cabinet. Strewn all about her were roses. Rain was lashing her window. By the clock on the stove, it was a little past six in the morning.

She had blacked out again. She had spent the whole night there on the floor. A sob escaped her, and Jess said softly, "Not again! Please not again!"

Slowly standing, Jess was taken aback to smell smoke. She scanned her kitchen and was stupefied to behold a half-smoked cigarette smoldering in the ashtray on her table. Someone had been there. Someone had been inside her apartment, standing over her while she was out to the world.

Jess looked down at herself, wondering. Ray

Porter's business card was at her feet among the scattered roses.

Quickly, Jess found her phone and punched Ray's number. His answering machine came on. After leaving a quick message, she snagged her purse and her jacket on her way out.

Large wet drops pelted Jess the moment she stepped outside, stinging her cheeks and neck. Fortunately, the rain stopped by the time she reached Pacific Avenue and was driving along the Presidio wall. She came to a stately home. The parking space in front of the garage was empty.

Jess checked the address, and slid out. The steps were wet and her shoes squished. At the top she froze. The front door was halfway open. "Ray? Hello? Anybody home?"

No answer came from the bowels of the house. Jess nudged the door with her toe and went in fast and low, her gun raised. She was in a hall, with the dining room to her left, the living room to her right. Ray liked a lavish lifestyle and extravagances only the rich could afford.

An eerie silence prevailed.

Jess searched the living room first. The furniture shone with new polish; the carpet was thick enough to drown in. The dining room was basically the same, with the addition of a crystal chandelier. But no Ray. She roved on down the hall. A closet contained nothing but coats and an umbrella. The next door opened onto basement stairs.

"Ray?" she shouted. Once again there was no answer. She was about to go down when faint music drew her to an alcove and a side door that opened onto the yard.

Jess stepped out onto a stone patio. Near it was a hot tub, and seated in the hot tub was Ray, his back to her, his arms outstretched. Jess lowered the Beretta and crossed toward him. "C'mon, Ray. I'm not jumping in with you."

Clothes were scattered about like he had undressed in a hurry to get into the tub. "You saw me drive up," Jess deduced, "and couldn't wait to spring into action. Didn't you get the message I left on your machine?"

Ray's monogrammed shirt was between Jess and the tub. Bending, she picked it up. "You can get dressed. It's not going to happen."

A sticky sensation on her fingers prompted Jess to look at the shirt again. It was splotched with blood. Aghast, she ran to the tub.

The back of Ray's right hand was turned toward her, and square in the center was a burn mark. The water in the tub was red. Another step, and Jess's fear became reality.

Ray Porter's face resembled chopped hamburger. He had suffered the worst beating yet—a beating so sadistically savage, there was nothing left of his nose or his eyebrows, and both cheeks were mashed to bits. His eyes were wide-open, mirroring the terror he had felt in his final moments.

Jess opened her mouth to scream, but someone beat her to it.

A maid was at the side door. Pointing at Jess, she shrieked, "You killed him! You killed Mr. Porter!" She darted back inside. "I'm calling the police!"

"You do that," Jess said numbly. First Bob, then Larry, now Ray. Whoever was out to make her life a living hell was doing a damn good job of it.

The house swarmed with law enforcement officers: uniforms, suits, CSI, photographers, the works. Alone at the heart of the maelstrom, Jess stood in the alcove, her arms clasped to her sides.

Dale Becker went by, his stare as penetrating as a laser. And he wasn't the first to give her that look.

Mike came from the patio. "So it looks like he was beaten and dropped into the hot tub. And he's got the burn on his hand."

"I know," Jess said.

"Let's hope that this time our killer slipped up and left us some clues."

She didn't know if she'd ever be optimistic about anything at this point. Lieutenant Tabor came through the door wearing his patent world-weary expression.

"So."

"So," Jess said.

"Ray Porter. You used to . . . date him."

There was no point in lying. They'd find out eventually anyway. And it would only hinder the case. *Her* case.

"Yeah."

Lieutenant Tabor aged five years, and Mike could see that he was going to lace into Jess about the latest coincidence, so he jumped in to protect her feelings and to keep everyone focused on the case.

"Okay, look, we got a good lead: a blood sample off victim number two. We're just waiting on the lab."

"When will you know?"

"Tomorrow hopefully."

Lieutenant Tabor looked around at the latest crime scene. He put his fingers to his temples and rubbed in small circles. "The newspapers are having a field day with the serial angle. Their reporters are snooping all over, digging up what dirt they can. It's only a matter of time before Inspector Shepard's name is brought into the spotlight."

Jess had never felt so alone, so small, so helpless.

"I'm sorry, Inspector," Tabor said to her, "but three strikes and you're out. We can't keep your involvement our personal secret. You have to go on the record, now. I've got no choice." He paused. "I would like for you to come to the station for formal questioning."

"Is that absolutely necessary?" Mike asked.

"Have you been listening to a thing I've said, Inspector Delmarco?" Tabor was at his irritated best. "Yes, we have to, to cover the department's butt, if for no other reason. She is integral to this investigation."

"I wish there were some other way, sir," Mike said.

"You think I don't?" To Jess, Tabor said, "I'm sorry. Truly sorry. I know you've been through hell, but the worst might be yet to come."

Jess almost laughed. "What else is new?"

Mike ushered her into the interview room, then left to get some coffee. He didn't shut the door. Jess heard the babble of voices in the squad room. She also heard something she wasn't supposed to: Lieutenant Tabor and John Mills on the other side of a two-way mirror.

"I still think it might be best if we just pulled her off the case," Tabor proposed. "For all our sakes."

Mills was his usual decisive self. "Do you have any material evidence on her? Anything at all to indicate that she killed these men?"

"No, of course not."

"I didn't think so. Just knowing them is not proof of a crime. Proof of bad judgment, maybe. But I'm not having her kicked off her first Homicide case. It'll kill her career."

"I just think it would be asking a lot of any inspector." Tabor did not sound happy.

"I'm not asking anything of you I wouldn't do

myself," Mills said. "She'll get through this. You'll see."

Mills could see that Tabor was not especially pleased with his answer. He didn't care. "She can handle this, and she's going to handle this. You can do your job and let her do hers." Mills spoke with a distant authority in his voice that let the lieutenant know who was in charge.

"I wish I shared your confidence."

"I've known her since the day she was born," Mills said. "Her childhood was hell. She grew up tough and she grew up strong, and she'll prove it if you give her a fair enough shake."

"What do you think I have been doing?" Tabor was offended. "I've bent over backwards for her. And I'll go on doing it as long as you want, despite my reservations."

"That's all I ask."

Jessica twisted in her chair to try to glimpse Mills as he left, but the angle was wrong. Resting her elbows on the table, she cupped her chin. Despair ate at her like an acid.

Mike reentered with two cups of coffee. He placed one next to her and sat across the table. "I guess we should begin." He reached over to press the RECORD button on the recorder. He hesitated for a moment and said quietly, "Listen, I'm sorry about last night."

"Let's just get this over with. Please?" Jess was understandably testy.

"It'll only take about five minutes, okay? Just the standard form."

"I know," Jess said. She didn't really want to be taking this all out on him, but he was in the unfortunate position of being there. "Let's go," she instructed.

Mike activated the recorder and slid a pen from his pocket. "For the record, give your name and badge number and current assignment."

Jess knew the routine by rote. She had never expected to be the subject of an interrogation, but mercifully, Mike kept it short by sticking to the essentials. She related her one-night stands with the three victims. She told about the clicking outside her apartment. But there were two things she didn't mention. One was her blackouts. The other was her darkest secret of all. The secret that could undo all Mills had done on her behalf and end her Homicide career before it started.

Her day wasn't over yet.

Another appointment with Dr. Frank had to be endured. Jess arrived early and sat in the waiting room in a state of dazed dismay until his secretary said she could go in.

Frank was in his chair, holding his clipboard. "You look positively terrible. No offense."

"You're no movie star yourself. No offense." Jess fidgeted in the doorway. "Tell me something, Doc.

Do you think it's possible to do things behind your own back?"

"What is it you think you've done?"

Jess sighed and sat down. "There's been another murder." She took out a cigarette, but didn't light it. She started to roll it in her fingers—her longtime nervous habit—but she was shaking so much she dropped it on the floor. Staring at it, she continued matter-of-factly. "And I'm my own best suspect."

"Says who? Your superiors?"

"Says me. I've thought about it and thought about it, and maybe I've been playing mind games with myself. Doing things when I didn't know I was doing them."

"Jessica, listen to me," Dr. Frank said. "You grew up all your life knowing your father had done these horrible things. So you think to yourself, maybe I have that in me, too."

"I don't 'think' I have it in me. I know it."

Dr. Frank stared at her. "Having thoughts about doing something isn't the same as doing it."

"Isn't it?" Jess stared out his wide window at the city's skyline. "I feel like I'm losing my mind, Doc. There's nobody I can trust." She had set the trap beautifully. Now all that remained was for him to take the bait.

"You can trust me."

The bald-faced lie brought Jess to her feet. "Trust *you?* When you have me sit here and spill my guts, telling me all this bullshit about a 'vault,' and then you go and talk to my partner behind my back?"

Dr. Frank took it all in: the accusation, the thought behind it, the anger expressed in it. He looked Jess squarely in the eye. "Is that what Mike said?"

"Well, it's true, isn't it?"

Frank chose his next words with care. "Jessica, my conversation with Inspector Delmarco had nothing to do with what you and I have been discussing."

Jess was in no mood to be forgiving. "Then what was it about?"

"You know I can't tell you that," said the doctor. He was unwilling to compromise his confidentially regarding any matter and, by showing this to Jess, hoped she would trust him.

But she didn't. Jess got off the couch and walked over to him. "Then what good are you?"

The two exchanged deadly stares. Neither was willing to give in even a little to the other's position. Making the final definitive statement, Jess turned and walked out without another word.

Jess had one more stop before she could call it a day.

The medical examiner's lab was a scientific wonderland. Long tables were lined with various apparatuses, not half of which Jess recognized. There was an optical bridge comparison microscope, a portable X-ray device, a time-lapse VCR, a comparator, magnifiers, and more. To one side was a cyanoacrylate fuming chamber.

Lisa Banks was at her work station, engrossed in a slide. "Well, look who it is," she said cheerfully. "Your partner has already been in to see me."

"He and I have been out of touch," Jess said. "Care to repeat yourself so I don't waste the visit?"

Lisa swiveled her chair. "The good news is I was right, as usual. That teeny drop of blood—no way it was from the victim."

A surge of excitement coursed through Jess. "So we have our killer's blood?"

"The bad news is he's not in the system. CODIS, the convicted felon database, got me zip."

"Damn."

"It's more than we had before, which counts for something. So . . . all you gotta do now is bring me the guy's blood who matches this sample."

"That's all?" Jess's despair surfaced anew.

"Yup. That's why they pay you Homicide guys the big bucks," Lisa cracked. "Surely you've got some good leads?"

Lisa moved to another part of the lab and fiddled with sophisticated testing equipment. She continued jabbering, not waiting for any answers from Jess. After all, she was used to not getting answers, spending most of her days with corpses. "Sometimes the clues are right under our noses and we don't see them because we're too caught up in what we're doing. Sometimes we have to step back and look at everything from a new perspective.

"Bring your pal Lisa a blood sample, my lovely, and I, one of law and order's little people, shall burn the midnight oil, doing tests, making the match telling you to lock our nutcase up," Lisa said. "You get all the glory. And what, you ask, do I get out of all this?"

Lisa finally realized that Jessica hadn't responded to anything she'd said. Her cynicism usually got some sort of rise out of the detectives. It was her way of letting them know she wouldn't be taken for granted.

"Jessica?" Lisa looked around the lab. "Jess?"

But Jessica was long gone.

CHAPTER 13

It was well and good to talk about looking at the case from a new angle, but Jess had been trying to unravel it for an hour without success. She was at the Palace of Fine Arts, near the pond. Two regal white swans swam past, so graceful and beautiful as to be surreal. Farther out were others. When Jess was little, she often wished she were a swan and not the ugly duckling she saw herself as.

The spot near the pond was one of her favorites. She came here often for the serenity. It was important she recharge her emotional batteries now and again or the weight of the world became too much.

A brisk gust fanned her hair and Jess looked up. The sky was still overcast. No rain had fallen since morning, but now a fogbank was moving in off the bay. Once it reached her, she wouldn't be able to see the pond, let alone the swans.

A sudden familiar clicking sent a shiver down

Jess's spine. She spun, her hand dropping to her gun, but it was only a photographer clicking photos of a wedding party. The bride and groom were Chinese. They, alone with the bridesmaids and grooms, posed for picture after picture.

The photographer moved to get a better shot and Jess realized she was in his camera's field of view. She couldn't say exactly why it troubled her, and she moved away from the pond toward the massive colonnades. The fog reached her before she reached them, swallowing her as Jonah had been swallowed by the whale. It was so thick, she couldn't see her hand at arm's length.

Jess couldn't hear the shutterbug anymore, either. Total quiet had descended, except for her own footsteps. She stopped to get her bearings and heard other footsteps behind her and to the left, slowly drawing nearer. Again, her hand flashed to the Beretta.

A commotion erupted, a series of grunts and what sounded like blows. Someone snarled, "You've been following me? I'll kill you!"

More blows landed as Jess warily moved toward the combatants. She passed several huge columns.

"I could have you up on report, you bastard!"

"Go ahead and try!"

The fog thinned enough to disclose Mike Delmarco and Jimmy Schmidt locked in a violent fight. Just at that instant Mike blocked a punch and gripped Jimmy by the shoulder, while at the same time hooking a foot behind Jimmy's legs. He threw the bigger man to the ground. Jimmy started to rise, but Mike thrust a finger in his face.

"Stay the fuck away from her, or I'll fucking kill you!"

Jess showed herself. "What *is* this?"

The two men were startled, then sheepish. Mike released Jimmy, who spat, "You two deserve each other." After glaring one last time at Delmarco, he hastened off into the fog.

"Well?" Jess said to Mike.

"I'm sorry about that. I caught that creep following you. My guess is he's been doing it all along. He's the one who has been playing you."

Jess slid the Beretta into her holster. If he thought that would satisfy her, he was mistaken. "How?" she asked.

"How what?"

Her hands on her hips, Jess stared him down. "How did you catch him following me unless *you* were following me, too?"

Mike had the aspect of a boy caught with his hand in the cookie jar. "Look, I'm just watching your back."

Through clenched teeth, Jess said, "Fine, but you don't have to mean that literally."

"You're being silly." Mike smoothed his shirt.

"Am I? Who showed up at the bar on the sly, scoping me out on the pretext he wanted to get a handle on his new partner? Who's been talking to my ex-shrink about my past behind my back? Who made a big stink about Ray Porter? And now Jimmy Schmidt?

Mike tried to put a hand on her arm but Jess wouldn't have it. "You've got everything mixed up."

Jess slowly backed away, saying, "I can watch my own back, thank you very much. Don't follow me again. Got that?"

"Please don't do this. I'm on your side."

Jess stopped. "From now on, *I'm* the only one on my side." Pivoting on the ball of her foot, she left him there in the fog and found her way to the parking lot.

Her apartment hadn't been disturbed in her absence. After bolting the door, Jess propped a chair against the doorknob and placed a half-full coin jar on the window's middle rail so if anyone tried to open it, the jar would crash to the floor and alert her. Then she opened a can of soup, put it on to heat up, and switched on the TV.

Jess tried to forget about the case for a while by watching a sitcom, but she didn't laugh once. Halfway through, she turned it off, sat at the kitchen table, and ate her soup. She didn't have much of an appetite, though. After a dozen spoonfuls, she bent her steps to her bedroom, and bed. She would get a good night's sleep, or attempt to, and be ready for whatever new catastrophes life had in store for her tomorrow.

But a few steps was all Jess took when the creak of a floorboard from the other side of her apartment door aroused her suspicion. Tiptoeing over, she listened intently, but heard nothing.

Then the floorboard creaked again. Someone was out there, lurking in the hall, and she doubted it was a tenant.

Jess silently moved the chair out of the way. She threw the bolt and yanked on the doorknob, only to find the hallway empty. Her mind had been playing tricks again, she thought, until she heard someone barreling down the stairwell. Whether it was the stalker or Mike or Jimmy was irrelevant. She gave chase, determined to put a stop to it once and for all.

Ordinarily, the stairwell was well lit, but someone had unscrewed all the bulbs between her floor and the ground floor. The only light filtered from above, and it wasn't enough to pierce the gloom.

The door at the bottom opened. "Halt!" Jessica cried, and heard the door slam shut. She came to the next landing and rounded the bend and had to clutch the rail when her feet became entangled and she nearly tripped.

The foyer was deserted. Jess hurtled from the building and looked both ways. A figure was disappearing into the fog. "Halt!" she repeated, and took hasty aim, but the figure melted away.

"Not this time." Jess flew in pursuit. Without any warning, a woman came out of nowhere pushing a baby carriage. Jess threw herself to one side to avoid a collision, and ran on.

"Hey! Watch where you're going!"

Jess heard cars go by to her right, but she couldn't see them. A fire hydrant materialized, giving her some idea of where she was. Skirting it, she stayed close to the curb. Presently, she came to the end of the block and had to admit defeat. Once again, whoever it was had given her the slip.

Jess retraced her steps to the fire hydrant. Because she couldn't tell exactly where her building was, she crossed the sidewalk and followed the row of buildings until she came to the stoop. Someone was using the elevator, so she took the stairs. At her floor she drew up short, appalled by the magnitude of her mistake.

She had left her apartment door wide-open.

Sidling along the wall, Jess peeked in. It looked safe, but she wasn't satisfied until she had conducted a thorough sweep. By now she was too tensed up to sleep. With the door once again locked and bolted and the chair once again propped against the doorknob, she filled her bathtub and let the hot water soothe her jangled nerves.

Jess expected to lie in bed for hours before falling asleep, but she surprised herself by succumbing within seconds of her head hitting the pillow. Exhaustion was its own reward; she enjoyed a dreamless peaceful night.

The reprieve was all too short.

Jess hadn't been up ten minutes when her phone insistently demanded she answer it.

"You can go right in," the commissioner's secretary said.

Jessica knocked anyway. John Mills's office was like the man himself, big and sprawling. Photographs covered the walls, broken here and there by commendations and plaques. Paperwork spilled over the desk like water over a waterfall, with case files everywhere.

"You wanted to see me?"

Mills had his jacket off and was working on a report. "Turn around and face the door, Inspector."

Fear spiked through Jess. Fear that her final secret was out and that she would be stripped of her badge and her gun and put on suspension pending an investigation. But she did as he wanted. "What is this?" she said, trying to make light of it. "Are you arresting me?"

"Test. The bulletin board behind me."

Jess didn't feel up to the challenge. "John—"

"Go," Mills said.

Closing her eyes, Jess envisioned the bulletin board. "Four thumb tacks at the top. Two red, two green."

"Three red, one green," Mills corrected her.

"Crime scene photos. Three black and white and two color."

"Two black and white. Three color."

Jess opened her eyes, startled. She turned around and saw that Mills was right: two black and white, three color. She'd gotten it wrong, which had never happened before. Jess could see that Mills was disappointed in her.

"Have a seat."

The chair Jess had sat in countless times, which once seemed so warm and cozy because it was in his office and he was the father she had always longed for but could never have, now felt uncomfortable and alien.

Mills folded his hands. "What is going on with you? You never fail that test. Never."

"There's a first time for everything."

"Spare me the clichés. Where is your head these days? Do you have a grip or not? I've been assuring Tabor you can hack it. Am I wrong?"

Jess squirmed uneasily. "It's more complicated than you imagine."

"What? You know a couple of victims, so you just let yourself fall to pieces? Is that it?"

She looked at the bulletin board. Complicated or not, he was right. "I guess I really am losing it, huh?"

"Hey, pull yourself together. You have a job to do."

Jess could only sit there and take her punishment. Admonition from John Mills was worse than a demotion. Besides, she knew he was right.

Mills stabbed a thick finger at her. "Since when are you a quitter? The girl I know, the girl I helped raise, never quit at anything in her life. When she set her sights on something she went after it with all she was worth."

"I remember her."

"Then reach deep down inside and dig her out. Show everyone what you're made of. Prove what I've known all along. That you've got what it takes."

Before Jess could reply, the door opened and in rushed Mike Delmarco. He took the other chair without looking at her.

"Inspector Delgato," Mills said.

"Delmarco, sir."

"You're late. Lateness is a sign of sloppiness. And sloppiness is one trait a detective can't afford, not on the job, anyhow."

"Sorry."

"Apology accepted." Mills looked at the two of them sternly. Then completely changed his attitude. The disciplinary action over, he turned his attention to the case.

"Well, let's get to it. I want to be brought up to speed on this case. Where are we? Who's on the suspect list?"

Jess and Mike glanced at each other. Who was

going to tell Mills what? And did they even agree on what they had at this point.

"There aren't any," Jess said.

Mike disagreed. "Aw, come on. It's that patrol cop. That Jimmy guy."

"It's not him. I feel it in my bones."

"Not who?" Commissioner Mills asked.

"James Schmidt," Jess answered.

"This guy," Mike said, pressing his case, "he knows police procedure, he's been following her, he's totally obsessed with her, plus he can't stand the fact that she was promoted. I say we just bring this guy in and—"

"Whoa, whoa." Mills was cautionary. "Easy there, partner. This Schmidt guy is a cop."

"Yeah?"

Mills bent toward Delmarco and spoke like a parent talking down to a wayward child. "You don't just accuse a fellow officer of something like this. It just isn't done. Unless you've got solid proof, this guy gets the benefit of the doubt."

"No," Mike admitted.

Mills focused on Jessica. "And you? What has this guy done that makes your partner think he's gone bad?"

"Followed me, like Mike said."

"That's all?" Mills knew her too well. "Or is there something you're keeping to yourself?"

"He broke into my apartment once, but it was no big deal. I sent him off with a bloody nose."

"He did *what?*" Mike demanded.

Mills was equally taken aback. He took a cigar from a cigar box and his lighter from his pocket, but put both down without lighting it. "Did you report this? And if not, why not?"

"Cops don't air their personal life in public."

Mills grunted. "Ordinarily, I would agree. But the core of this case is your personal life. At the very least you should have come see me."

"I'm a big girl now," Jess said stiffly.

"Then start acting like one. If this Schmidt does anything else, if he comes anywhere near you, follows you, anything at all, you're to let me know. And I don't mean maybe. Understood?"

Jess had to remember he was treating her like this because he cared. She nodded.

Lighting his cigar, Mills took a few puffs. "All right. That's a start. Who else is a possible suspect? Who else had access to all three victims?"

Mike Delmarco looked at Jess.

CHAPTER 14

The bar was familiar. Jess had been here once—a long time ago. It was dark and moody and perfect. She pulled out a stool and ordered a drink.

Jess was nervous. She hadn't indulged since Bob Sherman's body was found floating in the bay. But now the need was on her again, and she wanted someone. Wanted companionship. Wanted to end the aching loneliness for a few hours. Wanted to forget her ordeal.

A hunk of a guy in a studded black leather jacket strolled over and hungrily looked her up and down. "If you're here for what I'm here for, let's get it on."

"I like a man who knows what he wants," Jess said. "Let me finish my drink." She downed it in three gulps and a small atomic bomb detonated in her gut. "I'm set."

Jess threaded her way toward the exit. It hit her

what she was doing, and how stupid she was being. After Bob and Larry and Ray, how could she endanger someone else? So what if he was a complete stranger? She stopped. "On second thought, I've changed my mind."

"Oh, no, you don't." The guy pushed her. "Keep going."

"No." Jess wanted to avoid a scene, but already others were staring. "Forget it."

He pushed her harder. "Don't kid me. You want it, baby. You want it hot and hard. So move your tight ass before I move it for you."

Jess lost it. Emotion was unleashed deep within her, a roaring cauldron of rage and indignation and resentment. Her hand moved on its own, drawing the Beretta and pointing it at the biker. "Get away from me!" she warned, and to make him get away, she squeezed the trigger. As he fell, she saw his face clearly for the first time, and recoiled in shock.

It was Bob Sherman.

Another man came running out of the dark and flung himself at her. Jess fired again, catching him in midleap, and his body sprawled beside Bob's. This time it was Larry, a bullet hole between his eyes.

Now a third form leaped from the shadows. Jess whirled and fired, and she wasn't at all surprised to see that it was Ray.

One more face peered out of the darkness. She set to fire, and saw it was Mike staring at her.

Jessica sat bolt upright in bed, her body soaked with sweat. "God!" she breathed. "Not another one!" The nightmares were becoming worse. She sucked in deep breaths to steady her nerves and heard a *pat-pat-pat* on the window.

It was raining again. She glanced at her alarm clock. In half an hour it would go off. She pressed the button to turn it off. No sense in lying back down, she thought, because there was no way in hell she could get back to sleep.

Jess slid her back against the headboard and ran a hand through her hair. She wasn't looking forward to going to work—not with the ongoing tension between her and Mike. She wanted a new partner, one who didn't sneak around behind her back and pry into her personal life. But Lieutenant Tabor was bound to turn down her request.

A dripping sound drew Jess's gaze to the window. It was shut tight, the coin jar where it should be. Again, she heard the dripping. Only now she realized it wasn't coming from the window—it was closer, a lot closer. She glanced to her right just as a large red drop spattered on the edge of her pillow.

Jess's brain shifted into neutral. She sat as rigid as a board as drop after drop fell and a scarlet stain spread across the pillowcase. When the suspense became unbearable, she forced herself to raise her head. Inside the skylight shade, tucked directly above her bed, was a bundle of some kind.

Slowly rising, Jess stretched as high as she could and opened the shade. The bundle came tumbling out: a balled-up piece of clothing, dark red with blood. Some of the blood was caked dry, but the rest, where the rain leaking in the skylight had dampened the fabric, was wet and oozing more drops.

Jess was off her bed in a bound. Scooping the Beretta from her nightstand, she checked the door. It, too, was locked. From her nightstand drawer she took a pencil. A few pokes unraveled the mystery bundle. It was a shirt, an expensive shirt, with initials embossed in gold: RP.

"Ray's!" Her mind in a whirl, Jess backpedaled to the kitchen. Somehow the stalker had sneaked into her apartment. She figured it happened last night, when she stupidly left the door open.

The killer stuck the shirt up there to taunt her. There was no other explanation. The only thing was, Jess realized, that meant the killer had had the shirt in his possession a good fourteen hours.

Jess dashed to a kitchen drawer and took out a box of trash bags. Opening one, she slid the shirt into it and sealed the bag with a plastic tie. She opened her trash can to throw out the pencil because she didn't want to use it after it had Ray's blood on it.

Suddenly, Jess remembered Jimmy's bloody nose. From her silverware drawer she took a pair of tongs. The dish towel she had used to wipe up

Jimmy's blood was under the empty can of soup and some other garbage. She fished it out and slid it into a second trash bag, then put both trash bags in a brown paper bag and folded the top of the brown paper bag down.

Her right forearm was smeared red. Leaving the evidence on the kitchen table, Jess soon had her shower running and was standing under a blast of cleansing hot water. She scrubbed off the blood, and scrubbed some more.

Dawn streaked the eastern horizon as Jess pulled from the curb and tramped on the gas. As best she remembered, Lisa Banks liked to get to work early. Today was no exception. Banks was sorting some vials when Jess dropped the brown paper bag beside her.

"For me?" Lisa asked.

"I need a favor." Jess was shaky and not really sure she wanted the answers she was now asking for.

"Nice. Who from?"

Lisa pulled the trash bags out and opened them.

"Let's just say they don't know they're participating in this comparison study."

"I get it. On the Q.T." Lisa hefted the bags.

Jess smiled. "I owe you."

"Doesn't everybody?"

Jess spent the first hour of the new workday at her desk, getting caught up on paperwork. A third of a cop's life was devoted to filling out reports, and it was the third she liked least. She had two done and was starting on a third when the secretary bawled her name.

"Line four! DA's office!"

Wondering why the district attorney should be calling, Jess answered, "Inspector Shepard here."

"Jess, this is Kim Bailey. Remember me?"

"Of course." Bailey was an assistant DA Jess had met a year and a half ago when she'd found a homeless man with his throat slashed and had to testify in court. "What's up?"

"I need to talk to you ASAP."

"You make it sound like life or death," Jess joked.

"For you it could be. Meet me at the mall near the Hall of Justice, say, in twenty minutes?"

Jess promised to be there. Worry compelled her to arrive early. She was pacing to let off nervous energy when Kim Bailey hailed her.

Bailey was the consummate professional. She wore a suit and tie, carried a leather briefcase, and sported a sparkling gold watch. "I apologize for the cloak and dagger," she began, "but as soon as I found out, I thought you should know since it directly impacts our case."

"Which case is that?" Not that Jess couldn't guess.

"Haven't you heard? I'm prosecuting Edmund Culter. I thought it would be cut-and-dry until Ray

Porter popped on board for the defense. He's tough in the trenches. His death is a great loss to the legal community."

"He was one of a kind—that's for sure."

"Well, now one of the partners in Ray's law firm, Tim Wyngard, is taking over. And if anything, he fights dirtier than Ray did."

"What does this have to do with me?"

"The other side is building a particularly vicious defense. They're going for the throat." Several women were nearby, and Bailey motioned for Jess to walk with her so she wouldn't be overheard. "Your throat."

"What else is new?"

Bailey seemed to want to say something, but had to work up to it. "Jess, is there anything I need to know about your parents?"

Jess had expected something else. "My parents? What've my parents got to do with anything?"

"They're going to question your father's case in order to destroy your credibility. Somebody gave them a tip on your personal history."

"Come on. No way that's going to be allowed."

"That's not up to me."

Jess refused to believe it could happen. "Kim, you're prosecuting! You've got to nail this guy!"

Again Bailey hesitated. "I fully intend to . . . but . . ."

"But what?"

Kim Bailey was obviously not used to being spoken to in the accusatory manner that Jess was employing. Her temper was starting to rise. "But I've got a problem." She leveled her gaze so that Jess would grasp her full meaning.

She did. "Me? Oh, come on."

"Ray Porter's defense was built around your—how shall I say it—emotional problems."

Jess was trying hard to disprove that theory, but she found it hard to remain calm. "What are they saying? Where did they get their information?"

"Who knows? They have their sources just as we have ours. My point is that you have become a problem for the prosecution. Instead of just having to prove our case against Culter, we now have to rebut their case against you."

"Well, I did kick him," Jess said, "but they're taking it out of context."

"Maybe, but it still sounds solid." Bailey faced her. "Culter's sticking to his story, and in *his* story you lured him. Entrapped him."

"That's absurd." Jess clung to her lie.

Jess's emotions were fighting to take over as Kim Bailey pressed on. Was the DA enjoying this a little too much? Retribution for talking out of turn? Jess couldn't grasp the subtleties when the obvious was so distressing.

"And Ray had compiled quite a list of your—how shall I say it?—one-night stands."

Was she judging Jess now too? Bailey was supposed to be on her side.

"And they're saying that you threatened one of your fellow inspectors." The DA was relentless.

Jess was seething, but she used all the strength she had to keep it bottled inside.

Kim Bailey looked like she had sucked on a lemon. "You have no idea how hard you've made this. We'll be lucky to get Culter convicted of jay-walking." She consulted her gold watch. "Well, no sense caring about it. What's done is done. Now all I have to do is reassess our entire legal strategy and find character witnesses willing to testify you're not the sexual loose cannon the defense will claim." She started off, but stopped. "Do us both some good. Don't sleep with anyone else before the trial, okay?"

Jess rallied her sense of self-esteem. "Who I go to bed with—"

"Is none of my business, I know." Bailey said it for her. "But the defense might have someone watching you, waiting for another slipup. They know you're seeing Dr. Frank for anger management, and that your father—"

"Thank you, Kim. I believe we've already been over all of that. I know the problems. Just win the case," Jess instructed.

Once again, Kim Bailey reacted to the demanding tone of her client. "If you can stay clean long enough to let me, I will."

Jess could no longer face the reality of the situation in a calm, professional manner. Before the DA could light into her again, she turned and walked away. As she walked, she heard Kim Bailey's words: "Anger management. Your father. Entrapment." She saw Culter's face in front of her now. She could hear his words: "Your daddy's blood is pumping through your veins."

Could it be true? Could that maniac Culter be right? Was she as much a criminal as he was? Jess stared dazedly into space. It would all come out now. In court. In public. When it did, she could kiss her promotion, and her career, good-bye. She had kept it a secret because she was sure no one would take Culter seriously. It was her word against his. A police officer's against a lowlife's. But now the defense team might have enough on her to lend extra credibility to Culter's claim. Enough to have the case thrown out.

Jess shuffled into motion. It was all thanks to the leak, to whoever had provided the defense with her personnel file and was keeping them posted on the latest developments. Maybe it was a private investigator. Then again, maybe someone else was out to slit her throat. Someone who knew her.

The more Jess thought about it, the madder she became. Someone was setting her up—someone inside, with access to the case. She steamed about it all the way to Homicide, and when she arrived, she flung the door open so hard, it smashed against the wall.

Everyone froze. Mike was at his desk. Dale Becker and Sims were huddled together.

"All right." Jess stormed toward them. "Why are you doing this to me?"

Many of the detectives exchanged glances. Mike stood. Dale Becker laughed and whispered something to his partner.

Jess focused on Dale. "Someone in this room is fucking with me and I want to know who it is!"

Becker laughed louder. Jess started trashing his desk. "Whoa. Meltdown. Back off, boys. She's going to blow!"

"Cut it out," Mike said.

"Hey, your partner is the ditz going off the deep end, not me," Dale responded. "Maybe you should ask her to spare us the theatrics."

Jess homed in on him and was gaining speed when someone stepped from the lieutenant's office and stopped her cold.

"Jessica!"

The disappointment on John Mills's face was like a punch to Jess's stomach. She didn't say anything because there was nothing she could say. Nothing that would undo her lapse.

"We need to talk."

Mills took Jess's arm and led her out of the squad room. He settled them into his office. When he spoke, he couldn't hide his emotions. "Have you any idea what you've just done?"

"Made a fool of myself," Jess said weakly.

Mills carefully contemplated his next words. It was a while before he spoke. "It was an honor for me to raise you—you know that? To raise my partner's child. To do what he wasn't able to."

"All I ever wanted was to make you proud." A lump in Jess's throat nearly choked off her next words. "And I've let you down."

Mills took her hand, then ran a finger across her forehead, pushing her bangs back. "No. This is my fault. I pushed you too hard. I should have pulled you from the case, but I thought . . ." Mills tenderly clasped her hand. "You need to take a break. The case is not important. All that matters to me is your well-being."

Something in his look rang an alarm bell in Jess's head. He was being too condescending. He always pushed her hard—he'd just admitted as much. But no matter what, he kept pushing her. He wanted her to be tough. He wanted her to be capable. He wanted her to be a good cop. Just like her father had been—before he was pushed too far, perhaps?

Jess released Mills's hands. "You think I'm like him."

Mills seemed surprised by her statement. "What?"

"You think I'm like my father." She really wasn't sure if she said it out loud to convince him or to convince herself of the opposite. Either way, she ignored Mills's appeal to stay and bolted out the door.

CHAPTER 15

The parking lot was busy at that time of day. A lot of police cars and other vehicles were coming and going. Jess still had a few yards to go to reach hers when she saw something on her windshield. A single long-stemmed rose had been carefully tucked under the windshield wiper.

A note was attached. Jess opened the card and read aloud, " 'Guess who? I won't let that creep scare me off. I know you still care.' "

Jess gripped the stem. Jimmy Schmidt. It had to be. He was still pining for her. He refused to leave her alone, refused to make the break clean, like she wanted. "Damn him." She struck the hood with the rose, hitting it again and again and again, until most of the petals were smashed to bits or had gone flying.

Someone coughed, and Jess looked around to find a pair of uniforms staring at her. "What? You don't have anything better to do?" She cast the stem to the ground, climbed in her car, drove to the exit, and waited for a break in traffic.

Down the street, parked at the curb, was a white pickup. Jess could only see the bed and the rear of the cab. But as best she remembered, it was the exact type of pickup Jimmy Schmidt drove. The driver, who had his back to her, was staring into his side mirror, which afforded him a clear view of the parking lot.

"Bastard," Jess said, and when a gap in traffic materialized, she switched on her signal and turned into the other lane.

The white pickup suddenly lurched from the curb and rapidly gained speed. Jimmy poked his head out and grinned, as if the whole thing were a huge joke.

Jess gained speed. A confrontation was long overdue. She would end his harassment here and now and have one less worry to deal with.

At the next intersection, Jimmy wheeled left.

The light changed to yellow, but Jess turned anyway. He stuck his head out again, but he wasn't grinning this time. He seemed mad. She went a little faster and so did he. A car pulled out between them and Jess had to stamp on the brake pedal to avoid crashing into the other vehicle. The driver crawled along, delaying her, enabling the white pickup to gain half a block.

It was a no-passing zone, but Jess passed anyway. She whipped around the slow-moving car and barely made it through the next light before the red. Jimmy had turned again, and she did the same. He was sticking to the speed limit. She was content to follow because sooner or later he was bound to stop, and when he did, she would lay into him.

Their game of cat and mouse continued for over a quarter of an hour. Soon Jess divined that Jimmy had a definite destination in mind. He was leading her somewhere. At first she thought it was the Pacific shoreline, but then it dawned on her that he was making for Golden Gate Park.

Jimmy made a few more turns, winding toward the park's southwest corner. *Why there?* Jessica wondered. When he parked and got out, he smirked and beckoned, in effect daring her to follow him in on foot.

She did. Walking briskly, Jess pursued him along Martin Luther King Jr. Drive. To the north was the Murphy Windmill. Ordinarily, she would enjoy the gorgeous flowers and the leafy trees, but today all she cared about was Jimmy. He was walking so fast, the only way she would catch up was to run. But she chose to conserve her energy, and was content with keeping him in sight.

At the junction, Jimmy turned left. Every now and again he glanced over his shoulder and grinned. To him this was great fun. He had always struck her as immature, but not until that moment did Jess realize exactly *how* immature. He acted more like a teenager than a grown man. His crush on her had become a fixation and he just wouldn't let it go.

In fairness, Jess couldn't place all the blame on him. She had let him get close, had let him take her out, and later had let him make love to her. But she never, ever expected it to lead to this.

Jimmy turned right onto John F. Kennedy Drive. To the left was the Golden Gate Park Golf Course, where gaily clad golfers were enjoying their favorite pastime. To the south was the equestrian field, where several riders were putting their mounts through their paces.

The sun felt good on Jess's face. It made her think of the day she spent in the Marine Unit boat with Mike. A wonderful day, one she would long remember, yet it, too, had turned sour. Just like everything else in her life.

Jess gave a toss of her head. She refused to bog herself down in self-pity. She had spent far too much time lately moping about the state of her life. It was time she took control. Time she asserted herself. Time she showed that she merited Mills's trust.

Jimmy was still setting a marathon pace. Jess wondered where he was leading her. Golden Gate Park was huge, nearly three miles long and half a mile wide, encompassing more than a thousand acres.

North Lake appeared to the north. By then Jess's legs were aching. She used to jog regularly, but had stopped about six months ago. Still, she pushed on. She had come this far; she would see it through to the end.

Chain of Lakes Drive bisected John F. Kennedy Drive, but Jimmy stayed on Kennedy. He slowed when he came abreast of the bison paddock. The big beasts seemed to fascinate him. He pointed at them and motioned, but whatever he was getting at eluded her.

A group of tourists was coming the other way: dozens of Japanese with their cameras, clicking pictures. Jimmy melted in among them, and Jess lost him. She ran, giving the group a wide berth, confident she would spot Jimmy again once she was past them. But Schmidt had vanished.

Jess figured he had gone off into the trees, but on which side? She gazed southeast, toward the stadium. Then a prickly sensation at her nape caused her to turn, and there he was, forty yards away. The instant she saw him, he spun and moved deeper into the vegetation.

Jess went in after him. Once she was off the trail, she was in a whole new world. The babble of voices and laughter faded. She heard a robin warble and saw a squirrel scamper along a limb high in a tree.

Jimmy had chosen one of the most secluded spots in the park. He had to have been there before.

How else would he know about it? Jess rested one hand on her Beretta and her other on her *yawara*. She was taking no chances.

The ground was sprinkled with old leaves that crunched with every step Jess took. She tried not to make noise, but she couldn't move as quietly as she would have liked. Not that she believed she could sneak up on him. He was probably watching her right that second—watching and waiting for the moment of his choosing.

Proof came from a pocket of dense undergrowth a stone's throw to the northeast.

"I didn't think you had the *cojones*, little girl."

Jess stopped. The vegetation was a solid green wall, as impenetrable as fog. "Come out where I can see you."

"And have you shoot me? What's with the hand on your gun? You'd think I was a criminal."

Jess gave it to him straight. "I don't know what you are anymore, besides a royal pain in the ass." She had his position pegged. Or so she thought until he answered from a different spot.

"Come on. You still like me and you know it. I saw it in your eyes the other day."

"You're reading things that aren't there, Jimmy."

"Tell me you don't love me anymore," he challenged.

"I never did."

That brought a long silence. Jess glimpsed a

shadow but wasn't sure whether it was him or a trick of the light.

"You never liked me? Not at all?"

"I never said that," Jess replied, and realized it was a mistake the second it came out of her mouth.

"I knew it!" The undergrowth parted and out walked Jimmy. He had no weapon, and he was smiling as if he had just won a million dollars in the lottery. "So there is a chance for me."

"No chance at all." Jess had her hand firmly on the Beretta. "The sooner you get that through your mixed-up head, the happier both our lives will be."

"It's that Mike guy, isn't it?"

"Oh, for—" Jess couldn't believe his stupidity.

"Don't act innocent. I saw how you two look at each other. And you went to La Bodega together."

"Which proves absolutely nothing. He and I are partners." Jess fell silent. Here she was, justifying herself to a man who had stepped over the line more than once. "But that's not the issue here. *You're* my problem, not Mike Delmarco."

"What did I do?"

"You don't know how to take no for an answer. I told you flat-out I didn't want to see you anymore. I told you to leave me alone. To stop coming by. To stop calling. And what did you do? You've started following me. *Stalking* me."

Jimmy came closer. "You make it sound worse than it is. I gave you a bouquet of roses, and for that, you damn near busted my nose. I give you a rose today, and for that, you followed me all the way here to—" His eyes narrowed. "Say, why did you follow me, exactly? To ream me out?"

"We're not leaving here until you get it through that thick head of yours that we are through," Jess declared.

"Oh? What do you plan to do?" Jimmy held his arms out from his sides and continued coming. "Shoot me? Shoot an unarmed fellow officer?" He laughed. "I don't think so."

"There are other ways."

"Like bloodying my face again?" Jimmy shook his head. "Not going to happen. The last time you took me by surprise."

"Stop," Jess said.

But Jimmy Schmidt did no such thing. "Go ahead. Prove everyone right. It will make their day."

"What are you talking about?"

"You, babe. You're the hottest topic in the department right now. You and your string, that is."

Jess shouldn't be surprised, not given the number of people who knew about her love life: Mills, Mike, the lieutenant, Dale and his partner, the district attorney's office, Eddy Culter's defense team. Now that she thought about it, she was lucky she wasn't on the front page of all the newspapers.

"Guess I'm not the only one to ring your chimes, huh?" Jimmy made a clucking sound. "And here I thought you were pure as the driven snow."

"Go to hell."

"Hey, why get mad at me? I'm just repeating what's been making the rounds. Better you hear it from a friend than on the street, right?" Jimmy stopped a few feet away.

Jess was set to tear into him. "You're not my friend, Jimmy. You're not my lover either. You're a pathetic excuse for a cop, and you won't even be that much longer if I report this to your captain."

Jimmy sneered. "Go ahead. I'll just tell him how you picked me up that night and took me home. Just like all the others. Only difference is, I'm still here to tell the tale. You wanted me then. I'll tell them you wanted me now. Who do you think they'll believe?"

"I'd hope they'll believe me, Jimmy, because it's the truth. Yes, I've done some stupid things, picked up a few too many guys. But it doesn't mean I'm going to do it again, and it sure as shit doesn't mean I killed anybody."

"Well." Jimmy shrugged. "I don't want to be the one to test that theory. So keep your hands off the gun and just leave."

Jess let out an audible sigh. "I'm sorry, Jimmy. It just wasn't meant to be. Can you accept that?"

"Maybe. For now, anyway. Now go before one of us does something stupid."

Jess didn't look back. She just left him there, afraid of what he might have done. But more afraid of how she might have stopped him.

CHAPTER 16

Jimmy Schmidt may have been a little crazy, but at heart, he was a cop. He knew right and wrong. Besides, Jess had a gun. So after the taunts and the mere threat of his presence, he backed off.

Driving deliberately, she sped home as fast as the law allowed. She thought a nice hot bath would give her time to think as well as ease the weariness from her tired body. Jess filled the tub with steaming water and added bubble bath. After stripping, she took a bottle of wine and eased down into the bubbles, luxuriating in the warmth that spread through her body. Then, leaning her head back, she let her thoughts drift where they would.

It wasn't long before Jess was feeling a little light-headed. It didn't take much, she thought. The tension of the case, the day, her conversation with Mills, her confrontation with Jimmy—two sips of wine and she was almost giddy.

Then a faint *scritch* from elsewhere in the apartment nipped her good mood in the bud. Now alert, Jess sat up, sloshing water and bubbles over the side. She strained and heard the sound repeated.

Common sense dictated Jess investigate, but when she tried to stand, her legs were unsteady.

The sound came again, louder now. Jess suspected it was from the skylight, that someone was trying to break in. Forcing herself to focus, she propelled herself out of the tub and into a robe. She moved stealthily down the hallway and grabbed her gun from its holster, which was hanging on the back of a kitchen chair.

Her apartment had gone quiet. Moving slowly down the hallway, Jess girded herself and stepped into her bedroom. Her skylight was fine. "Now I'm hearing things," she mumbled.

No, she wasn't, because the sound came again, from the living room. Jess turned too fast and paid for it with a wave of dizziness. One hand against the wall, she came to the end of the hall.

The front doorknob was twisting back and forth. Someone was trying to break in.

Jimmy! Jess thought. As quietly as she could, she grabbed hold of the chair she had propped against the knob and slid it to one side. Then, her finger curled around the Beretta's trigger, she jerked the door open and thrust her pistol directly into the face of . . . Mike Delmarco.

"You?" Jess blurted.

Mike had been trying to get the door open with a credit card by sliding the card between the door-jamb and the casing, a trick Jess only ever saw work in the movies.

"Thank God you're okay."

Jess held the Beretta level. "Why wouldn't I be?"

Farther down the hall there was a low sound, like the scuff of a shoe. Mike glanced back, uncharacteristically apprehensive. "Jess, something's wrong. The feeling you had that someone's been following you? I've got the same feeling. Like something's going to happen tonight."

Jess stared at the shadowy doorways. Could it be Jimmy out to pay Mike back? she wondered. Her mind wouldn't focus. She couldn't make a clear case for anything.

"Jess?" Mike asked, seeing she was not her usual confident self.

And she wasn't. She didn't know whom to trust. Including herself. Still training the Beretta on him, Jess backed inside. "Get . . . away from me."

Mike turned his back to her and threw the bolt. "You can put that away now. We're safe."

"No one is safe around me," Jess said. "Least of all me. Keep away or back out you go."

Mike started toward her. "Don't treat me like this."

"*Stop!*" Jess cried. Her every nerve was taut as barbed wire. She centered the sight on his chest, her trigger finger trembling.

"Jesus, Jess. Careful with that thing or you're liable to blow a hole in me."

"A whole lot of holes if you don't stay right where you are."

To complicate matters, the wine was having more effect. Jess's thoughts were becoming jumbled. Her body felt sluggish. The Beretta weighed a ton. She couldn't hold it much longer.

"Jess, I'm on your side. Always have been. Please stop pointing that thing, will you?"

Not because he asked, but because her arm was leaden, Jess lowered the pistol to her side. "Go away."

"Why?"

"Everyone dies . . ." Jess tried to make it to the sofa, but her legs weren't ready to take her that far. An arm slipped around her waist, and she stiffened as Mike pulled her to him.

"You can't even stand up."

". . . who touches me," Jess said. She feared the consequences, but she craved the human connection.

Mike sniffed a few times and frowned. "Jess, you've been drinking too much. Gotta stop this. Stay strong." He touched her cheek.

"Mike, no," Jess said. "No . . . don't . . ."

"You're making no sense." Mike stroked her wet hair.

Jess tried to draw away, but she was too weak,

too confused. "Everyone who kisses me turns up dead."

Their eyes locked. Jess's head was swimming and her heart was fluttering, but whether that was from the wine or from the whirlpool of conflicting emotions seething within her, it was impossible to say.

"No, they don't," Mike said, and bent his mouth to hers.

Jess had never been kissed like this before. A kiss so exquisitely tender, she yearned for it to go on forever. It might have, too, except that a few seconds later a rectangle of light speared the room, impaling them in its pale glow.

Mike stepped back. "What—"

The old Chinese lady was staring in at them.

"My neighbor. She watches me." Jess slurred her words. She plucked at his shirt. "Don't go, Mike."

"I'm not going anywhere, stranger."

Jess heard him as if through a long tunnel. His face became fuzzy and the room faded to a twilight gray. She felt her legs go, felt his arms slide under her. He lifted her and placed her on the sofa. She wanted to thank him, but her vocal cords wouldn't work. Her robe fell open, and through slitted eyes she saw Mike staring down at her. At her thighs. His hand came toward her.

Jess's breath caught in her throat. She was helpless, exposed, vulnerable. If he was the stalker, here was a golden opportunity he couldn't pass up.

But all Mike did was pull her robe close about her. Then he sat with his back to the sofa and drew his gun.

Jess couldn't decide if he was staying there to protect her or if he had another, more sinister purpose. The living room faded to black. She was unsure how long she was out. When she opened her eyes, Mike was still by the sofa. She watched him a bit, until she drifted off once again.

More time passed. Jess was suddenly awake. Her blood had stopped flowing and she had little strength. Enough, though, to crack her eyes open.

Mike was still on the floor by the couch, her special box next to him, where she had left it. If she had known she was going to have company, she never would have left it in the open. Never left it for anyone else to see. He was somewhat respecting her privacy by moving things around with the tip of his gun, or was that just so he wouldn't get his fingerprints on anything?

He spotted the photo of her father after the suicide and studied it for a while. Mike looked at the photo and then back at Jess, not realizing she was looking back at him through slitted eyes.

Jess never let anyone see that. Not even Mills. She had taken it from a pile she had found in Mills's den shortly after he had taken her in.

Mike moved a few other things around in the box with his pistol, but left it basically undisturbed.

To his mind, she would never even know he'd looked inside. She was obviously out cold.

And even though she tried with all her might to rouse herself, Jess couldn't fight the fog overtaking her mind. Once again she passed out, this time to sleep the dreamless sleep of the dead.

Whether it was the sunlight streaming in her window or the ringing of her phone that awakened her, Jess didn't know. Sitting up, she glanced around the room, but Mike wasn't there. Her mouth felt as if a bird had built a nest in it. Fumbling toward the noise, she retrieved her cell phone. "Hello?"

"Hi. It's me, Lisa."

Jess stepped into the hallway. "Mike?" she called out.

"Mike? Jessica, it's Lisa. You okay?"

"Huh? Yeah," Jess said.

"Look, the reason I'm calling is about those two blood samples. You wanted to be notified as soon as I had the results."

"Does one of them match that drop of blood you found on Larry Geber?"

"Sorry. No match on any of those samples you brought."

Jess leaned her forehead on the wall. "Thanks. I owe you."

"Not at all. Anyway, let me know if you've got any more for me," Lisa offered.

Any more? Jess wondered if Lisa thought she was running a blood bank.

Jess clicked off and went to the living room. "Mike?" He was gone. He had left her sometime in the night, alone and defenseless, after rifling through her things.

A tide of worry brought her to the box in a rush. She verified that all the photos and everything else were accounted for.

Jess replaced the box in the closet and headed to the bathroom. She looked a mess—a walking zombie with skin too pale and her hair sticking out at all angles. She thought about Lisa's phone call. So Jimmy Schmidt definitely wasn't the serial killer. She never seriously considered him a suspect, but she had requested the test on his blood to be sure.

The investigation was at a standstill. Jess had no one left to test. Or did she? she wondered, and looked at her reflection again. According to Jimmy, half the department believed she was the killer. With all her blackouts, who was to say they weren't right?

Jess opened her medicine cabinet. Her razor was on the bottom shelf. Several washcloths were on the rack, including one she hadn't used yet. She spread it out on the sink, held her left index finger above it, and pressed the razor to her skin. A quick slice and the deed was done. Drop after drop fell until she had a red ring the size of a fifty-cent piece. From the medicine cabinet she took down a box of Band-Aids and applied one to the cut.

The drive to the medical examiner's office seemed to take five times as long as it should. Jess couldn't stop thinking about Mike. She couldn't understand why he had left her in the middle of the night. Anyone could have broken in, and she would have been helpless.

Lisa Banks was surprised to see her. "Don't take this personally, my dear, but you look like hell."

Jess handed her the plastic bag containing the washcloth. "I need this right away."

Taking it, Lisa said, "Right away takes twenty-four hours."

Jess gripped Lisa's arm. "Lisa, please. I need it."

Lisa glanced at her hand, at the Band-Aid on Jessica's finger. "Okay, I can skip a couple of steps and run it straight through the amplification process. Then do the full test later."

"Thank you." Jess needed to know, once and for all. "How long?"

"My, my. You *really* want these results, don't you? The rush job will take a few hours, but I hope you realize it increases the chances of an er—"

"Can I wait in your office?" Jess requested.

"Sure, hon. Be my guest."

"I owe you. Again." Jess turned.

"You know," Lisa said, trying to cheer her up, "I

always say, you can tell a lot about a person from a drop of their blood."

"Yeah? Can you tell if they're a good person?"

Lisa was opening the plastic bag. "Can you give me a while?"

CHAPTER 17

Jessica paced for a while, then sat at a desk and rested her head on her forearms. Even though she'd slept, she was so god-awful tired she couldn't think straight. She blamed it on the stress, the constant strain of being on edge. Soon some of that stress would be relieved, one way or another.

Not meaning to, Jess dozed off. A chaotic dream disturbed her rest, horrific images of corpses and blood and something off in the dark going *click-click-click*. The pressure of fingers on her shoulder woke her.

"Hey, Earth to Neil Armstrong?" Lisa kidded.

"I fell asleep."

"No fooling. You okay? Want a cup of coffee?"

"No, thanks." Jess saw a sheet of paper in Lisa's other hand. "So—"

"Sorry," Lisa said. "No match."

"Really?" Jess was ready to burst into tears of

happiness. Then Lisa laughed and clapped her on the arm.

"Naw, I'm kidding you. Congratulations. You've got your killer."

The walls spun and the floor heaved. Or so Jess thought as she put her hands on top of the desk and slowly stood. For a few dizzying moments she feared she would pass out. But the spinning stopped, and crestfallen, she shuffled toward the door.

"Are you okay?" Lisa asked.

"You have no idea," Jess said. She had forgotten to say thanks and was going to turn around, but she heard Lisa pick up the phone, so she just kept walking. Her body was a numb husk drained of all vitality, all emotion. By rights she should be a wreck. She should be blubbering and wailing. But all she felt was a great, terrible emptiness inside.

Jess wasn't conscious of reaching her car and starting it, or of driving aimlessly, mile after mile. She no longer seemed part of the world around her. She was detached from everything, adrift in the emptiness within her. She might have gone on driving for hours and hours, but the strident screech of a gull penetrated her haze and brought her crashing down to Earth.

Somehow, Jess had wound up near a beach. She parked and got out and walked along a footpath to the sand. A man and two boys were flying a kite and a woman was walking a dog.

Jess sat on a driftwood log and stared out over the gently lapping waves. Her mind was in neutral. She didn't think, barely blinked, simply sat and stared. Her thoughts were a riot of memories and mental groping. Mainly about her father. How ironic that she had, quite literally, turned out to be a chip off the bloody block.

She was a serial killer.

Jess's blackouts were now explained. She had read about people who committed murders and later claimed they couldn't remember doing it, and she always chalked it up to a ploy to escape prison. But now she had a whole new perspective. She had murdered these people, and she honestly and truly and sincerely couldn't remember.

Poor Mills, Jess thought. After all he had done for her, after taking her in and raising her as his own and doing all he could to further her career, she had betrayed his trust and his love. There was that word again: *betrayal.* She had accused so many others of it. Yet another irony that she should be guilty of the worst betrayal of all.

In a way, Jess was glad she didn't have a family. Glad she could spare loved ones the heartbreak, to say nothing of the stigma. Now that she thought about it, she realized that the only person in the whole wide world who truly did love her was Mills. Once she was behind bars, she would hardly ever see him again. It heightened her empty feeling. Never in her entire life had she felt as terribly, unbearably sad as she did at that instant.

All things come to an end, and eventually Jess's numbness faded. She saw with some shock that the sun was sinking and that she was the only one left on the beach. A brisk breeze had picked up, sending shivers along her body.

Jess didn't want to go back. She didn't want to confront the horror of what she had become. But it had to be done.

On the drive to her apartment, Jess pondered her choices. The way she saw it, she had two: she could confess to Mills or the lieutenant, or she could throw herself off the Golden Gate Bridge.

Suicide was out. Ever since her father killed himself, Jess saw that course of action as the coward's way of dealing with life's cruelties. She never felt pity for those who succumbed. She only felt contempt.

That left giving herself up. It was the right thing to do, the decent thing to do, the smart thing to do. But Jess balked. Once she did it, her life as she knew it would end. There would be a trial, which the media would turn into a sensationalistic circus, and if she were lucky, she might get life instead of the death penalty. Or maybe a clever lawyer could have her committed.

One more night, Jess thought. She wanted one more night to herself. Tomorrow was soon enough. Tomorrow morning she would phone Mills and have him meet her in Lieutenant Tabor's office, and that would be that.

Surprisingly, Jess was hungry. She stopped at the supermarket and bought a lobster and a few gourmet items. It would be the last fine meal she ate for a long while, and she should make the most of it.

Jess didn't place a chair behind the door or her coin jar on the window. Why bother, when the killer was the face that stared back at her from the bathroom mirror every morning?

A bottle of wine was left from the night before. She drained what was left into her glass. She chopped lettuce for a salad, opened more wine, diced a tomato, drank more wine.

A light came on in the building opposite. Jess turned and saw the old Chinese woman watching, as always. Pouring more wine, she lifted her glass in a mock salute. "Who knows what you've seen over there?"

As if the old woman somehow heard, her lights went out.

The alley was plunged in darkness again. Jess saw her reflection in the windowpane—and something else: Jimmy Schmidt, standing in the kitchen doorway behind her. With a gasp of surprise, she whirled.

"Hello, Jess darling." Jimmy drunkenly wagged his lock pick at her, then slid it into a pocket. "How are you doing?"

Jess was incensed. "What the hell are you doing here?"

"I came for forgiveness." Jimmy started toward her.

"You came to the wrong place." Jess had put the Beretta and her *yawara* on the table. He was backing her into a corner, but she might be able to reach them before he reached her. Suddenly she was weak and dizzy.

Jimmy guessed her intent and scooped up her *yawara*. "I want you to forgive me."

Jess needed a weapon. Anything would do. She backed against the counter and groped behind her. Her fingers brushed a slender object and nearly knocked it into the sink. Catching it, she realized it was the pair of scissors she had used to cut the roses. "Jimmy, get away from me. Go home."

Jimmy moved the *yawara* in a slow, threatening circle. "Go home? What am I, your dog? You want me to obey you?"

"I want you to go!" Jess whipped the scissors around. "So help me, if you don't, I'll cut you."

"Try," Jimmy dared her.

Even though he was drunk, Jess was no match for him in her condition. He was bigger and stronger, and she was woozy from the wine. She sidled to the left, then bolted for the kitchen doorway. He didn't try to stop her. She made it to her bedroom but her legs were buckling, her vision blurring. Slamming the door, she locked it and staggered to her bed. She needed to sit down, to rest a moment. If she didn't she would collapse.

"Knock, knock!" Jimmy rapped on the glass panes of the door and laughed.

"Go away, damn you."

"You're supposed to ask, 'Who's there?' " Jimmy said. When she didn't, he finished the joke himself. "Knock, knock. Who's there? Lover. Lover who? Your lover boy, babe, come to patch things up."

"Leave me alone!" Jess tried to stand, but her body was tingling and her limbs wouldn't work. It dawned on her what was happening. "Not again!" she breathed, feeling herself ooze onto the bed and unable to do anything to stop herself. "Go away, Jimmy! *Please!*" she begged

Crash! A pane of the door broke from the *yawara*. Jimmy's hand reached in through the broken glass, searching for the door handle. Blood from his cut hand dripped down. *Crash!* A second pane smashed.

Jess tried to lift the scissors, but she was too weak even for that. Blackness had engulfed her senses. Dimly, she thought she heard the strange clicking sound she had heard on other occasions.

Then there was nothing, nothing at all.

The feel of someone pressed against her back was the first thing Jess became aware of. Momentarily confused, she opened her eyes. She was lying on her side in her bed, fully clothed, her head on her pillow. An arm was draped over her shoulder. An arm she recognized as Jimmy's.

Jess twisted her head. Jimmy's was buried in the other pillow. He hadn't molested her, hadn't done anything other than tuck her in and fall asleep.

Out on the street, children were laughing and squealing. They almost drowned out the wail of sirens. Jess felt something under her hand and looked down. It was the pair of scissors. Jimmy's hand was next to hers, and on the back of his *was a fresh burn mark.*

Terror struck, Jess sat up. "Jimmy?" She nudged his shoulder. When he didn't respond, she slowly rolled him over. Her fear soared to new heights.

Jimmy Schmidt had been beaten to a pulp. His face had been savaged to the point where his own mother wouldn't be able to make a positive ID. He was worse than Bob had been . . . worse than Larry and Ray Porter. The pillow under him was soaked with blood.

Jess opened her mouth to scream, but froze at a tremendous crash from the living room. Boots pounded in the hall and there were more crashing sounds. The next moment burly members of the SWAT team, in full gear, burst into her bedroom and trained their SMGs on her.

"Holy shit!" one bawled into his headset. "We've got a body! Repeat, we've got a body here!"

Jess started to stand, but the men were on her in the blink of an eye, two of them seizing her by the arms while a third expertly frisked her. A gun muzzle was shoved in her face.

"On the floor! Now! NOW! Do it now!"

Jess knew the routine. One of the SWAT guys straddled her and roughly jerked her arms behind her back. Handcuffs were slapped on her wrists.

"She's in the bag!"

"Go easy on her," a familiar voice said.

"Easy, hell!" another SWAT member said. "Take a look at the bed. That's a *cop* she's killed this time."

"We don't know for sure she did it," the familiar voice said.

"Are you blind, Inspector?"

Jess looked up.

Mike Delmarco was in the doorway, his hands in his pockets, his face downcast. "I'm sorry it had to be this way, Jess."

That made two of them.

A lot of what happened after that was a blur. Jess was hustled into the back of a police car after walking a gauntlet of SWAT and fellow officers who looked at her as if she were the vilest scum who ever drew breath. She was driven to headquarters and taken into the same room in which Mike had recorded her statement. Only this time, it wasn't Mike who questioned her. This time it was Chip Marshall of the Special Investigations Unit. He was polite and professional, but his demeanor left no doubt what he thought of her. After a few preliminaries, he cut to the crucial questions.

"Now then, Inspector Shepard," Marshall placed a photo of Bob Sherman on the table. "Where were you the night of September twenty-fifth? The night Bob Sherman was killed?"

"I don't know," Jess answered.

"Don't or won't?"

"The truth is, I don't know. I suffered some sort of blackout and can't remember what I did that night."

"That's convenient." Marshall placed a photo of Larry on the table next to the photo of Bob. "And the night of October first, the night Lawrence Geber was murdered?"

Jess wanted to shrivel into the chair. "I don't know."

Another photo joined the others. "The night of October fifth? The night Ray Porter was killed?"

"I don't know."

Marshall looked at her. He added a fourth photo: Jimmy Schmidt's ghastly remains. "You don't remember doing this?"

Jess shook her head.

"I see." Bending toward her, Marshall said, "Jessica, be honest with me. Did you kill these men?"

"I don't remember." Jess was trying to hold herself together, but the four brutalized faces were too much. She started sobbing and couldn't stop.

"I'm sorry. I'm sorry. I'm sorry," was all she

could say. Was it to the dead men in the photos or to Marshall or to Mills? Jess didn't know anything anymore.

Chip Marshall stood. "Inspector Shepard, I must inform you that you will be formally charged with four counts of first-degree murder." He collected the photographs and put them in a file and walked to the door. "And off the record, allow me to say that I hope to hell you fry."

Jess was disappointed no one came to see her those first few days other than her court-appointed attorney. Not even John Mills. She lay on her cot in her cell hour after hour, glumly gazing at the blank walls. She rarely slept; she had no appetite. The jumpsuit she had been issued, two sizes too big and stiff with starch, made her skin itch.

Finally, someone did come. "I thought you might have some things you want to get off your chest," Dr. Frank said.

Jess stayed on the cot. "What's there to say? I was raised to be a 'good girl,' but I was born to bad people."

"Your lawyer was by to see me. He says you were suffering from blackouts. Why didn't you ever mention them to me?"

"Oh. I see where this is leading. You'll make a great witness for the prosecution," Jess said.

"All I've ever wanted to do was help you."

"You did a great job."

Dr. Frank grew defensive. "I did my best. I can't be blamed if you wouldn't open up to me."

Jess shrugged. "It's okay, really. Kind of comforting, in a way. I've been running from it all my life. Fear of being the bad seed." She took a deep breath. "It's good that I'm in here, Doc. It keeps other people safe."

The door swung open with a jarring *clang.* John Mills stood there with a document of some kind in one hand and an overnight bag in the other. "What are *you* doing here?" he growled at the psychiatrist.

"I've been counseling her, as I'm sure you know."

"Is that what you call it?" Mills entered the cell. "But this works out fine. Now I can ask you to your psychobabble face."

"Really, Commissioner, petty insults become no one. Don't fault me for trying to help her with her problem."

"If you're as good as you think, you would have seen the truth," Mills said.

"Seen what truth?"

"Have you been giving her any medications?"

"I've given her nothing."

"I didn't think so." Mills shook the document. "The problem is not in her mind. It's in her bloodstream."

"*What* was in her bloodstream?" Dr. Frank demanded. He did not like being verbally battered by Mills.

"Forensics report. I had them run her blood sample through a drug screen. Rohypnol. Ever hear of it?"

"Yeah, of course. The date-rape drug. It's completely incapacitating." Dr. Frank reached for the report, but Mills didn't give it to him. "Are you saying someone has been drugging her?"

Mills tossed the overnight bag onto the cot. "Get dressed. You're out on bail." He turned to Frank and dismissed him. "Thanks anyway. We won't be needing you anymore."

Overcome with amazement, Jess sat up and opened the overnight bag. It contained her clothes and purse. "Where are we going?"

"Where else? To nail the son of a bitch who did this to you."

CHAPTER 18

New energy flowed through Jess as she matched John Mills's long strides. "I can't get over this. I was drugged?"

"Wrap your mind around it and move on," Mills commanded. "Give me the headline. And don't tell me you're not up for playing games. This is the 'game' of your life, Inspector."

Jess nodded in agreement. Her entire future was at stake. "Four men were killed. The suspect slept with all of them. Incriminating evidence was found on her person the morning after the crimes."

"When she awakened from 'drug-induced' blackouts," Mills pointedly amended, "which makes it physically impossible for her to have committed the crimes."

"God," Jess said, and stopped. The full impact hit her and her eyes moistened in pure joy. "I didn't do it."

"Time later for celebrating," Mills advised. "Stick to business. The case remains the same. Only the suspect changes." He resumed walking.

"Who?"

"You can answer that yourself, but you refuse to," Mills snapped. "What do the victims have in common?"

"Just me."

"And who knows the most about your habits? Whose job is it to know where you are at all times because he might have to reach you at any hour of the day or night?"

Jessica stopped again, then had to hurry to keep up. "You're off on that. Mike never knew where I went at night."

Mills bestowed one of his paternal looks. "Didn't it start when you got the new job? When you *met* him?"

"It's not him," Jess said, but her conviction had cracks.

Just then they emerged from the building. In the distance lightning flashed and a few seconds later there came the rumbling boom of thunder. A deluge was battering San Francisco. Jess bent her head against the lashing rain and shrieking wind and ran with Mills to his car. She slid in on the passenger side.

"Gimme some directions here," Mills said as he pulled out. "I'm waitin' for you to tell me where to go."

Jess rattled the directions off and immediately asked, "But why would he drug me?"

"How better to keep you out of action while he was busy doing what he had to do? Think he'd let you prowl, without following you?"

"But how did he know who I slept with?"

"Come on. Take off the blinders."

Jess peered into the downpour, her heart as heavy as lead. "There *were* times I thought I was being followed."

"Suspect followed the accused. When? Where?"

"The night she picked up a man at a bar."

Mills grunted. "Then maybe back to the victim's place, where he could've even seen what was going on. Through a window, the crack of a door." He leaned on the horn so a slow-moving SUV would get out of their way. "Enough to drive him crazy!"

Jess gulped. Mills had a point. None of it had started until after she met Mike Delmarco.

"I'm waitin' on you, Inspector! Got somethin' to say?"

"Suspect had intimate knowledge of the habits of the accused," Jess related. "Access not only to her premises, but to her deepest fears, plus familiarity with the drug that ultimately incapacitated her."

Stating the facts like that caused tears to form in Jess's eyes. It wouldn't have seemed possible, but she just made the case. Mike was setting her up.

Mills popped his glove compartment and

pointed to the tissues. Jess gratefully took one as
they barreled on toward Mike's place.

Mills took a turn on screeching tires and
grinned. "It's like being with your dad again. Except for the tears. You didn't get the worst of him,
Jess. You got the best of him." He gently squeezed
her arm. "It's like having my old partner back.
Cruising the streets, cross-checking the facts, recon-
structing the case, and drawing the bottom line."

"It's all just circumstantial," Jess said. "You
know that we don't have enough to arrest him."

"Unless we can provoke him into giving himself away." Mills flicked the windshield wipers
from low to high. "I called ahead and told him
you got out because you have evidence of who the
killer is."

It was all going too fast, Jess thought. She
couldn't keep up with events. "When was this?"

"Right before I bailed you out. We want him
nervous. We want him to sweat. I also told him
you're due back in the DA's office to give sworn
testimony tomorrow." Mills was in his element. "In
my estimation, it would be in his interest to try to
stop you."

"Wait a minute. You set me up as bait?"

"I figured you wouldn't mind some payback."

The truth was, Jess wouldn't, but she wished
Mills had consulted with her first. "Do you think
he bought it? My having evidence?"

Mills grinned. "We'll find out soon enough."

Fog shrouded the shoreline, but hadn't quite reached Mike Delmarco's house, which was perched over the water like a roosting bird of prey. Somewhere a sea lion barked. Out on the water a foghorn blared.

Mills checked the magazine to his Beretta, chambered a round, then holstered the gun and strode down the walkway. "Let's go, Inspector."

"Remember," Jess said, "he's a cop. We give him 'benefit of doubt.'"

"He's gonna get all the benefits he deserves."

Blues music drifted from inside. Mills marched to the front door and hammered it so hard, it was a wonder it didn't crack.

The music stopped and Mike called out, "Just a second." He was slow in opening up. His clothes were a mess, he hadn't shaved in days, and his eyes were bloodshot, either from too little sleep or too much alcohol, or both. On seeing Jess, his face lit like a Christmas tree.

"Jeez. Jeez. Ohmigod, I'm so happy . . ."

Mills wasn't having any of it. "Happy . . . yeah, yeah," he said, brushing past Mike. "You *look* so happy."

Mike was obviously confused, but he didn't try to stop Mills. He pulled Jess inside and hugged her.

"Glad I could make your day." Jess peeled his fingers off her and Mike stepped back, still confused and more than a little wary.

"What's the matter?"

"Why didn't you come see me, Mike?"

"They questioned the hell out of me," Mike explained. "I swore up and down you were innocent."

The refrigerator slammed. Mills had taken out a bottle of wine and placed it on the counter.

"Yeah?" Jess snapped. "How could you be so certain?"

"Whaddya mean? It's you, Jess. We're partners. And partners—"

Jess cut him off. "Partners lie for each other?"

While the partners continued their heated confrontation, Mills stood with his back to them. He took out three glasses and poured wine from the bottle he'd found. He turned toward Jess and Mike with a look that indicated he was now ready to rumble.

As Mills approached them with the wine, Jess continued her litany. She was in "test mode," the frame of mind Mills trained her to adopt to report any and all facts that would make her case.

"Or how about 'partners tell the truth to each other' or 'partners tell each other everything?' And what else? Oh, yeah. 'Partners come to see you when you're in jail.'"

Mike looked surprised, but she thought he could have been faking it. "You got my message, right?"

"There was no message from you," Jess spat.

"Whaddya mean?" Mike was now a little too unhinged to be a cool killer, but Jess couldn't see it.

Besides, cool killers were good actors. "And when I tried to come, somebody put me on the no-access list."

This was Mills's cue. "Looks like you were drinking some wine before we got here. Celebrating something?"

"Yeah, Jess got out."

Mills had placed the wine in front of them and returned to the kitchen. He rummaged through the drawers. He yanked open one after another, rifling the contents.

"What the hell are you looking for? What's going on here?" Mike asked.

Mills came over, his smile downright mean. "We're celebrating with you." He gave a glass to Jess and another to Mike. "Oh, let me propose a toast. To Jessica." In a single gulp he drained his glass. "That a problem for you, Mike?"

"Problem? Why should it be a problem?" Mike still didn't drink though. "Something going on here? You two playing some kind of joke?"

"You gonna toast, or what?" Mills demanded.

Mike looked at Jess. Whatever was up was not going away until he played along. He raised his glass. "Here's to ya, Jess." He slugged some wine. "And to you too, sir. Glad you were able to talk some sense into those assholes." He swallowed more wine.

Mills started to join him, but lowered his glass and just watched Mike.

"So what's up?" Mike asked calmly. "Say something, one of ya."

"Rohypnol," Mills said.

"Rohypnol? Yeah, and . . . what?" Mike couldn't figure the connection.

"Ever hear of it? The date-rape drug?"

"Yeah, of course, I know. Roofies." Mike took a step back and glanced at his glass.

"Oh, yeah. Roofies. That's what you hip guys call it." Mills snapped his fingers. "Hey, didn't you have a little girlfriend who died or something from OD'ing on that stuff?"

Mike wiped a hand across his forehead. He shivered, yet he was sweating profusely. "I don't want to talk about that. It's bad enough I have to see Dr. Frank now and then. I've always blamed myself."

Jess glanced at the Post-it on the wall. "That's why you have his number?"

Mills was watching Mike. "So you oughta know what roofies do?"

Mike took another step toward where his shoulder holster was draped over a chair. "Do? Jess, what's going on here?"

"Somebody was following me since these murders started. Somebody was drugging me all along." Just saying it made Jess mad.

Shaking his head, Mike said, "Whaddya mean? Who? How?"

"Somebody who was following me. Somebody

who was lurking around. You know, somebody who was in my place."

"Come on," Mike said. "You can't mean me?" He took another step, but his leg wobbled like he was drunk.

Mills was over by the drawers again. "Those roofies. Totally incapacitate you, don't they? Give you confusion." He put his hand in a drawer. "Feeling any confusion, Mike? How about anxiety?"

"You put something in my wine," Mike said.

Jess did a double take. "He did what?"

Mills held a small bottle up for them to see, his handkerchief around it. "Say, Mike, you got quite a stash in your drawers there."

"Stash?" Mike asked. "What're you talking about?"

"A little of this stuff must go a long way," Mills said. "Planning to date rape a whole herd of buffaloes?"

Mike pressed a hand to his forehead. He tried to focus and make sense of the words, but it was getting harder to accomplish. "What are you . . . ? Planting evidence? That's not . . . my stuff. Never . . . had that . . . shit."

Mike tried to reach toward his gun, but his feet were like lead. Mills didn't turn around, sure of the condition of his suspect. He knew where Mike's gun was, and he knew Mike wouldn't get to it. "You gonna pull a gun on us now, Mike?" Mills let

Mike know he didn't have to see everything to know what was happening.

Mills put the bottle back in the drawer and wrapped the handkerchief around something else. "Lookee here what I found. Right in the drawer, a what do you call it, a *yawara*. One of those little Japanese sticks that'll pound your features to pulp. Never had them in my day." Mills grinned at Mike. "Heard you were an expert with these things." He examined it. "What do you know? This little baby's got blood on it. Wonder if it's poor Jimmy's? Didn't much care for him, did you? Seem to remember you threatened to kill the poor bastard."

"No!" Mike backed up another step. A wild look came over him. "Not . . . mine! No!" Suddenly, he threw the wineglass to the floor and spun toward the chair, reaching for his gun.

Jess beat him to it. To her, his guilt was self-evident. He was trying to cover himself by denying everything, but that was typical. Most convicted felons denied committing a crime. Snatching his Beretta from its holster, she raised it to bash him over the head. "You prick bastard!"

In a flash Mills was there, holding her arm. "Easy. No bruises. Take our time, do this right." He grabbed Mike, who was on the verge of collapse, and lowered him into the chair. "Think ahead. Always think ahead. We're in this together. Partners. Now you understand at last. Yes. Just go slow, sweetheart."

Jess was grateful he stopped her. She lowered the pistol, content to let her mentor take care of things.

Mills stepped to the counter and fished a cigarette from a pack Mike had left there. Again Mills used his handkerchief. He wedged the cigarette between Mike's lips and lit it. Mike was too befuddled to resist; his eyes were rolling in his head.

"We've got a cop killer here," Mills said. "A man who's committed a very special crime, which requires a very special form of justice."

Jess wasn't sure what Mills was driving at, and said so.

"Stick with the master and I'll show you how it's done." Mills removed the cigarette and put it in a nearby ashtray. Then he lowered Mike's chin to his chest.

The scene was exactly like the one in the photo Jess had of her father. A twinge of apprehension knifed through her, and she asked, "What are you doing?"

"Make sure the crime scene is consistent with a suicide. First step, see that the room is clean." Mills winked. "Don't you touch anything, darling." He gathered the wineglasses, walked to the sink, and rinsed them out. Then he took a paper towel and mopped up the small amount of wine Mike had spilled. "Two, no sign of restraints or external struggle. Three, motive. Here, I'd say maybe remorse for what he did. Hopelessness."

Deep inside Jess an invisible hand twisted her gut into a hard knot. "John?"

Mills wriggled Mike's wallet out, opened his own, and transferred a photo of Jess to Mike's. "Unlucky in love works good, too." He replaced Mike's wallet, and stood. Palming his Zippo, he stood back and inspected the entire room while clicking the lighter. "All our prints have been wiped except the door and I'll do those on our way out. Tomorrow, those crime scene boys show up and . . ."

The truth dawned, the full, terrible, paralyzing truth, and Jess finished the thought. "A photo tells it all."

Mills smiled his mentor smile. "Exactly. Nothing as persuasive as a photo. Tells the whole story. And there's no messy court appearances. No chance of some asshole judge letting him out on bail." He stopped clicking his lighter. "Let's wrap this up." Opening Mike's unresisting hand, he held out his own. "Give me his weapon. What do you think? Handsome guy like this, he'd probably go for the chest. Not want to wreck his face for everyone to see. Okay, now let's have the weapon."

Jess looked at the gun, then at Mike and finally at John Mills. All their years together, all the times Mills had been there for her, his devotion and caring, it had all been a lie. This was the worst betrayal of all. Betrayal, and more. Adopting a two-handed grip, she pointed the Beretta at the man she loved more than any other. "Get away from him."

"What are you doing?"

"What they pay me to do."

"Of course. Don't you understand?" Mills was incredulous.

"Understand what?" She fought the tears, but they streamed down her face.

"I'm doing this for you," Mills continued.

"Get down!" Jess commanded. The pain of having to subject him, of all people, to simple police procedure almost outweighed the duty. Almost. "Hands behind your head! Do it *now!*"

Mills, ever the teacher, tried to coax his pupil one more time. "First rule: Gotta be crazy to be a cop," he said.

Jess thought the current situation certainly proved that true.

"Old saying," Mills continued. "Everyone runs away from a guy with a gun—cops run toward him." He looked straight at Jess. "Give me the gun."

His look was withering. She was used to obeying his voice. Years of conditioned reflex fought the present situation.

Mills saw the conflict in her eyes. "You won't use it, Jessica."

Another test? She'd failed one already. She was not about to repeat her failure. "On your knees!" she ordered. "Do it!"

"Your father had the same rage you've got," Mills said quietly, still trying to take control of the situation.

"You killed my mother," Jess answered just as calmly.

"Your father killed your mother because I told him. I had to tell him. You tell your partner everything! I told him about her and that hippie scum she was playing around with. He went crazy. Ran into the house. I heard screaming . . . yelling . . . then a shot. Then another! So damn sorry I got there too late. My whole life . . ."

"You're lying!" Jess cried out. "You've been lying my whole life long!"

Mike Delmarco picked that moment to lurch from his chair and bolt for the front door. He was past Jess before she could stop him.

"Mike, no!" Jess cried, but he wasn't about to listen. Too late, she heard footsteps, and swung around.

Mills was already on top of her and shoved her violently to the floor. "We can't let him get away!"

"Stop!" Jess shouted. But in another second Mills was outside, and there was a loud crash. She raced after them, and was dismayed to find the fog had moved in and swallowed the house and its environs. There was no sign of either man. Sprinting to the pier, she probed the pea soup for some glimpse.

Thinking Mike would make for the nearest

house to phone for help, Jess moved toward the street. The splash of what might be a paddle whipped her around. The fog thinned for a few seconds, and she saw that a skiff, which had been tied to the pier when they arrived, was gone. It had to be in among the pilings.

A piling loomed, then another, both encrusted with grime and salt residue. Jess's feet and lower legs were soaked, but that was the least of her worries. For a few seconds, the sea lions were silent, and she heard a thump from close to shore. She moved toward the spot.

Out of the fog came the *click-click-click* of Mills's lighter. Jess waded faster. The sea lions had started up again and she hoped the racket they were making would drown out the small splashes she made.

The skiff was drawn partway out of the water. Mike had managed to paddle to the wharf and pull himself up onto the landing. He was on his back, weak and helpless from the drug. Beside him crouched Mills, who had just burned the back of Mike's hand with a cigarette. As Jess looked on, Mills flicked the cigarette into the water.

Mike tried to speak but couldn't.

"I'll enjoy doing you, boy. Even more than the others. Because of you, she knows the truth." Mills produced a *yawara*. "You're not the only expert with this. I've yet to meet a man I can't beat."

His talkativeness gave Jess an idea. She hoped he would keep it up for another thirty seconds.

"Why?" Mike croaked.

"Why you?" Mills shrugged. "I needed a scapegoat for Jess. Why the others? They put their filthy hands on her. Violated her. I'm just sorry I only discovered what she was up to about a month ago. There must be a lot of others who deserve to die."

Mike tried to prop himself on one elbow. "You're sick," he said.

"Because I look after those I care about? That's not sick—that's love. Everything I've done, I've done out of love."

Jess was ready. She waded onto solid ground, the Beretta extended in her right hand. "It ends here, John." She could tell she'd taken him by surprise. Good.

"You killed them all," Jess said. She advanced another step, her left hand close to her side so he couldn't see what she was holding.

Mills stood riveted to the spot. He didn't even look at her. He just spoke words he'd made himself believe.

"Darlin', don't you understand?" Mills asked. "All of those guys weren't good enough for you and her. They were scum. Not like your father or me. You have that same emotional problem. You have her disease. I've tried to save you."

"You 'saved' my mother by killing her," Jess stated flatly.

"She was ruining my life. She was ruining her life and ruining your father's life," Mills said.

"My father's life!" Jess could no longer control her anger.

Mills faced her now. It was finally time for a confrontation. And only one of them would make it through alive.

"He couldn't give her what she needed. He couldn't stop her catting around. He made me do it," Mills said.

"You slept with her? You betrayed your partner?"

"She made me do it!" Mills was back in another time and place now. "She needed me. I loved her! I couldn't let her keep doing those things. It was the only way."

"Love?" Jess couldn't understand how love figured into any of this. Especially murder. No, once Mills started, he obviously liked the violence, the death. "You couldn't stop killing, could you?"

"Stop?" Mills thought about this. When he spoke again, Jess heard none of the avuncular warmth that had always greeted her in his voice. Good times or bad. "I stopped for all these years. And I could stop again. Control, Jess. It's all a matter of control."

Suddenly, a weapon was in his hand, a .38 snub-nosed revolver Jess had forgotten he carried in an ankle holster as a backup.

He reached his free hand out. "Give me the gun. I kill you, I kill a fleeing felon. You kill me, you commit murder."

A thin, tinny voice seemed to come out of the

fog. "Commissioner! Listen to me. You don't need the gun!"

Mills jerked back, then glanced wildly about. "Who the hell?"

"Test," Jess said. "Identify the voice now speaking to you."

"Where did it come from?" Mills was completely baffled.

"Think about this," the voice said, trying to talk Mills down. "Let's think about this."

"Recognize the voice of Officer Wilson Jefferson, my old partner?" Jess showed him her other hand; in it was her cell phone. "The miracle of speed dial. He's heard every word. So has Lieutenant Tabor and a lot of others."

Wilson's voice crackled from the phone. "Go along with the program, sir."

"So you think I'm beaten?" Mills said. "You think you have me outsmarted?"

"Give her the capture, Commissioner," Wilson urged. "Resisting won't get you anywhere."

Jess wished Mills would put down the revolver. The longer the standoff continued, the greater the likelihood one of them would take a bullet. "Maybe those 'asshole' judges will cut you some slack," she offered.

Jess suspected that Mills knew he was beaten. The student was now the teacher. But he had one more lesson left. Somewhere in his addled sense of right and wrong, he knew it would be wrong to kill her. So there was only one "honorable" solution. They called it "suicide by cop." Get the good cop to kill you.

Before she could blink, Mills jammed the revolver against Mike Delmarco's head. "Final test."

"No!" Jessica warned. "I'll shoot!"

"You'll never do it! Your father couldn't do it either. You're just like your father. Your father had no balls at all."

"How's this for balls?" Jess said, and squeezed the trigger.

The impact flung John Mills off the pier and into the bay. He hit with a tremendous splash among the sea lions and sent them into a frenzy of roaring and baying. For a few seconds his body floated, but only a few. Then he slowly sank into the black water, bubbles gurgling in his wake.

Jess went to Mike and took his hand in hers. He had passed out. Sitting on the sand, she carefully cradled his head in her lap. Eventually, the sea lions quieted and moved away, and then there were just the two of them, alone in the fog.

She was almost sorry when the black and whites and the ambulance and other cars arrived. Wilson was there, lending his support. Lieutenant Tabor gave her the thumbs-up. Dale Becker and Sims and others from Homicide formed a protective ring around her and Mike. She was one of their own now.

At the center of the commotion, Jess looked down and found Mike staring at her.

"Mills?"

"Gone."

"I'm sorry." Mike's eyelids fluttered. He was barely conscious, yet all he cared about was her.

"No, *I'm* sorry. I thought you were the guy."

"I *am* the guy."

"You are the guy," Jess confirmed.

"I'll see you later, stranger," he whispered, barely conscious.

"See you later."

Jess knew this time it was true. And it was good. She let Mike know all of that with the smallest of smiles—the last thing he saw before he blacked out.